The Tale of
Asa Bean

Other books by Jack Matthews

Hanger Stout, Awake!
Bitter Knowledge
An Almanac for Twilight
Beyond the Bridge

The Tale of
Asa Bean

Originally Titled *Fabula Fabuli,*

But Changed after Admonishment and
Correction of the Author by the Publisher,
as having chosen a Title of too Great an
Irrelevancy to that Public Whose Imprimatur
is Deemed Essential to Literary Excellence,
and which Title Signifies a tale about
one Asa Bean (himself Irrelevant according
to the Many), whose Wit (*ingenium*) is
Unnaturally High, whereas his Judgment
(*judicium*) is Naturally Low, and whose Story
is Accordingly Found to be a Human one

by Jack Matthews

Harcourt Brace Jovanovich, Inc., New York

In memory of the Rev. Bjørn Johannsen

I believe he would laugh often and heartily
if he could read these pages.

Such, says Imlac, are the effects of visionary schemes: when we first form them we know them to be absurd, but familiarize them by degrees, and in time lose sight of their folly.

—*Rasselas*

The Tale of
Asa Bean

1

The bearded Anarchist, dressed in a coat three sizes too large and inhabiting the crepuscular frames of an old newsreel, paces restlessly up an unwatched street, holding a homemade bomb deep in one pocket, and a fistful of sulphur matches deep in the other. A cold wind blows up the street, and the world totters in this madman's vision, while a voice whispers to him, through the tattered veils of thirty years, "Now is the time!"

A Shawnee brave steps quietly toward the edge of a clearing, where a man hoes corn, trying to tame the Great Bitch, Earth; and the Shawnee grips a short, strong bow in one hand, an arrow notched and ready. The Shawnee looks briefly past the laboring man at a cabin from whose chimney a thin stream of smoke flows upward into the warm dusk. The rectangular solidity of the cabin vaguely disturbs him, and he turns his eyes back to the man who stands in the young corn, working.

The Assassin lifts a blind in some distant building, and gazes out upon a street that will become infamous in history. He lifts his rifle and peers through the telescopic sight, already imagining the target coming into view. The target has become an imitation man, moved electronically, and the thought of its efficiency and power infuriates the man with the rifle, who has vomited twice already this morning and knows that the world will make him even sicker before the day is over.

2

I am standing beside the statue of Boadicea and her hounds in front of the building. Behind me, there are twenty steps; before me, there are nine. Let it be said: I am on the side of Boadicea.

I stand on the twenty-first step, and go up on my toes, flexing the gastrocnemius muscles in the backs of my legs. I can see the top half of my body in the massive glass doors ahead. I am wearing my red ski cap and a U.S. Navy pea coat that I bought at a discount store four months ago. I see before me the upper half of a bearded man, looking a little like Starbuck (I think), or maybe it's Stubb. Anyway, he could be one of the *Pequod*'s crew. I like this fantasy. (I think it's Stubb.)

This fellow has an absolutely expressionless face as he stares back at me. He is inscrutable; and knowing what's behind this face, I am tempted to shout with laughter and tumble backward down the twenty steps. It's hilarious, but I don't make a sign. I breathe out long scarves of steam that flap about my head. It is eighteen degrees outside, but sunny.

This is enough crypto-narcissism. I have work to do. I walk up the remaining nine steps, and walk toward the doors that whip open to let me enter.

Fanfare of silence.

The same dumpy little guard, dressed in a blue uniform

4

(the exact color of my pea coat), rests tired, familiar, ancient eyes upon me as I walk past. The weight of his vision is almost imperceptible, but I am aware that he is regarding me.

I walk past, climbing more steps as I approach the foyer that connects the front display chambers. Marble all about me, great livid columns holding up a dull lavender paisley ceiling some thirty feet overhead. My steps resound in this great hallway.

Move on, Crypto-Narcissus, for you have work to do.

Yes, it is true. *This may be the day.*

I think of the Anarchist, the Shawnee and the Assassin. In my right pocket, I fondle a jackknife with a pearl handle. I bought this in a second-hand store.

My footsteps echo, and I whisper to myself, "Onward, Asa M. Bean. Onward, for there are all those rich canvases waiting with all those rich painted colors on them, depicting rich statesmen and rich ladies, rich generals and rich courtesans (and rich crypto-courtesans). These are the fatted calves I can sometimes hear lowing in my sleep."

Yes, I literally say these things to myself. I talk to all things, and to all people, which, of course, includes me. Usually I speak softly, so they (we) don't hear. But we (they) must keep on talking.

Today may be the day.

I am filled with excitement, and my palm sweats as it (female symbol) holds the knife (phallic) in its warm (female), uncompromising (female) grip (female).

I pass by the first great entrance, looming with soft darkness, like the ancient Caves of Alongoza, which—it was said—gave off an odor of peppermint, whose cool and fragrant drafts would cause a match to burn with double intensity.

The Caves (female) of Alongoza (female).

5

Inside this room, standing motionless upon the cool marble, are two young girls whispering quietly to themselves as they stare at a painting of Louis XIV.

Today may be the day!

I walk past; and halfway down the hall toward the next room, I do a quick pirouette on my right foot. Now, when I stop, I am standing between two statues: one is of Mercury, the other of a fawn. I am somewhere in between.

Today may be the day!

The Anarchist, the Shawnee, and the Assassin and Myself do not fully understand this building, but we are nevertheless delighted to reject it for intellectual reasons.

Now another guard appears from a distant room, and he is walking slowly toward me in the hall. His hands are clasped behind his back, and he is stooped and old, and I know his face well: it is the face of an elderly gray rabbit—eyes too far apart, and a swollen undifferentiated muzzle. But he wears the uniform of a guard, and a cap that stands Gestapo-high above his forehead.

I approach him slowly, my heart beating in my throat.

Somewhere in the distance, I hear a resonant whistle and an echoing yell. School children are being shown through the museum. At this instant they are near the vomitorium at the side.

I enter the next room and go to the four-sided bench in the center and sit down. The amber vinyl cushions are pneumatic (female). I am hungry, and I take my naked hand out of my pocket (female) and gaze at it.

Circling me on four sides are early cubist paintings. Their silence is overwhelming, and it roars out from the walls upon my ears, carrying with the insistent noise the odor of dried-up bubblegum.

School children now inhabit this secret and august place.

6

Through the doorway to the next room, I briefly glimpse a young man and woman (female), as they pass by, holding hands and gazing peacefully at the paintings. The woman's glance briefly flicks over me as I sit there silent and alone. It is no heavier than the breath of a grasshopper as it flies past your face.

I sit and brood for fifteen minutes. Then sixteen minutes. Seventeen.

Then I make up my mind: today is not the day. I haven't even faced the problem of which painting to choose.

Tired and discouraged, I stand up and make my way out of the museum.

Asa Bean, the Ironist, has experienced another epiphany. He needs irony as all divided men need it; or, being ironic, he needs division.

Thus continueth the cycles in the perpetuation of their figures.

Leaving the art museum, I remove my ski cap and rub my hand through my hair. I am distinctly relieved. Then I drop my cap, lean over and pick it up.

Standing erect, I perceive that the world is exactly as I remembered it an instant before. Although it is getting dark: shadows are beginning to float past the buildings like sudden cold lakes in the air. Two cars pass by with their headlights glowing.

Somewhere in the darkness (the winter days end halfway through the afternoons, it seems), the Anarchist, the Shawnee, the Assassin and Myself stand and laugh at me.

3

Asa M. Bean, the Minister's son, stands aloof upon the cold, windy street corner, hands in pockets. One hand rattles change; the other hand clasps a large, ancient, loose-jointed jackknife (or clasp knife, or pocketknife). Asa Bean is remote from the pavement upon which he stands. The pavement is covered by ice that looks like a sheet of dented lead.

Asa Bean narrows his eyes and watches traffic pass by. Asa Bean (sometimes known as "Asa M. Bean") is an existential hero: the only stationary figure in a world of burbling flux. Like Archimedes, he knows the lever and he knows the fulcrum, and will someday pry the world loose.

Asa Bean, the latest avatar of Heraclitus, stands still amid the confusing and alien storm. He looks up and stares God in the face, seeing that one of the celestial eyes is bloodshot— Betelgeuse, the great red star, beloved of Joseph Stalin and Vladimir Kropotkinov.

Fumes and stenches rise in a Coptic dance, and beetle juice flows poisonously in the gutters, reflecting the stars from its gumbo waves.

Asa Bean notices all, and analyzes the corruptions of the world, melanomic and sorrowful (female), and treads upon thin ice.

Of course, the gutters do not flow with resins and bile: they are frozen, and their corruptions glow upward, back at the sacred stars, insolent (the gutter serums) in their human provenance.

Only Asa M. Bean's blood flows, and only the traffic flows.

All else is paralyzed in this bark of time. Catatonia, catatonia, what makes your big head so hard?

Asa Bean sings this evening song, his mind flexed like a delicately poised sparrow, upon a forgotten marshmallow of truth.

Asa Bean, a man in search of himselves, sings, dances and orchestrates.

Asa Bean, *c'est moi.*

4

"Hey, Soy Bean!"

The voice is immediately recognizable. The nickname, too. Up on the tracks, a yard engine crashes into a lettuce car, triggering the ponderous latches. The sound reverberates up and down the tracks, and rattles the stage machinery all about.

Beyond the loading docks, illuminated by naked bulbs in green reflectors (stylized luminous pistils in stylized petal sheaths) every thirty feet . . . beyond the loading docks, and above, the lettuce car is nudged forward by the yard engine, its diesel growling with profound terrene menace, so that I can feel the throbbing in the soles of my feet.

"Hey, Soy Bean!"

The warehouse is still dark. A slumbering imploded city of groceries and produce and building blocks of Great Northern Tissue, reaching to the gray skylights. Before the tracks, there is a straggly line of luminous cattails, jutting up like mussed hair toward the first whisper of light.

"Hey, Soy Bean! You gone deaf or sumpn?"

I turn around, and there is Durango, standing by the

dark door. His hands are stuffed in the front pockets of his jacket, and he's dancing from foot to foot. ("Cold as a whore's heart, man!") His swarthy face almost evaporates in the gloom.

"You gone sleep out there?" Durango asks. "Out there in the fuckin cold, man?"

"Good morning, Durango," I say.

"Good mornin, shit," he says, dancing sideways like a boxer, but with his hands still snug in his jacket pockets, like two slipped and bony tits.

The lettuce car has stopped, and the yard engine is peacefully idling with a deep cacophonic rattle.

"We gotta unload that fucker?" Durango asks, jerking his head at the track.

"I don't know," I tell him.

"Shit. Bust our balls on them goddam lettuce crates."

The headlights of a car flash over us, and Durango says, "About time them fuckers get here and open up. Sfreezin out here!"

The car stops and the lights go off. Wilbur and Tubbs get out of the car and come toward us.

"Hurry up unlock the fuckin door!" Durango yells. "We damn near froze waitin here, you dumb shits."

"Hello, Durango. Hello, Soy Bean," Wilbur says. "That lettuce car for us?"

Tubbs looks up at it and breathes, "Shit!"

"Don' see no order," Durango says.

Then Wilbur opens the door, and a tropic breeze, warm with spice and mixed grocery odors and cardboard breathes out upon us, and we step inside.

"Mama," I say out loud, but no one understands or pays attention.

Wilbur says, "Soy Bean, go on up the front office and see if

10

that lettuce car's gotta be unloaded. Order oughta be on the board."

I start back into the darkness, through the roadways between the stacks, stopping at every fourth post to switch on another constellation of lights. I look at my watch after the first turn. It is nine minutes after 5:00 A.M. Like God, I am bringing this city to light.

Asa M. Bean strolls forward into darkness, pausing only to produce a world with a touch of his fingers. Archipelagoes of lights. Messianic and proud, he responds to the potent symbolism of his humble task—the only one in the whole warehouse who understands the miracle.

Rounding the corner of what he considers his personal row (where there is a section of 140-pound bean sacks lying in soggy inertness, like corpses after the battle), Asa Bean almost walks into a fork truck, looming there in the darkness. He sees the vertical chains first, glinting in the tenebrific aisle, and this saves him from cracking an ankle against one of the pair of insidious prongs thrusting out at the bottom . . . prongs which slide into the concavities of wooden pallets (female), and lift the pallet load tottering toward the ceiling (or merely a foot from the cement), and go wheeling with the load, dexterously fitting it on a truck, or stacking it ceiling high, under the sky lights.

The workmen are like ants in this colony of groceries and goods. And the fork trucks, which are painted an oddly bright blue, are called "bugs," reinforcing the insectival character of our essential tasks.

Cold as hell, outside. Three below zero during the night.

Asa M. Bean sings, "Massa's in the cold, cold ground," and flicks on another football field of illumination, showing the cardboard city that has been waiting for him all through the darkness. Miracle upon miracle.

Warmth circulates in drafts and eddies down the avenue. Asa Bean pauses to appreciate the serendipity of design. He contemplates what a fire would look like roaring through all this closed and silent world.

The Anarchist, the Shawnee, the Assassin and Myself stand still for a moment, singing old-fashioned barbershop quartet songs.

Then Asa Bean steps out with a smart salute, and plucks the unloading order from the board. The front office is dark inside the windows. A house within a house. The three women secretaries and the two male office workers will not appear for another three hours yet. Then the lights will be on, and the lettuce car in back will be unloaded.

Asa Bean returns to Wilbur, Tubbs and Durango. The yard engine is purring like a tamed triceratops in back of the loading docks.

Asa Bean returns victorious. Somewhere.

Burdened with so much irrelevant learning it is ironic that Asa Bean should work in the produce section of a warehouse. But then learning serves irony; and what *is* Asa Bean if not an ironist?

5

After I get off work at the warehouse (1:30 P.M.), I went home and took a nap. I woke up, tasting sleep and tiredness. Now I brush my teeth with Crest toothpaste, and rinse my mouth well.

Downstairs, all is quiet. The refrigerator hums and vi-

12

brates gently. The fridge is warm and moss-green outside; cold and cream-colored inside.

Bean the Vandal stands before the fridge and contemplates. Then he reaches inside and pulls out a can of Miller's High Life, the Champagne of Bottle Beer. He pops the can open, and takes a long gulp. Then he goes into the front room and sits on the corner of the sofa.

He remains an alien in this house, even after five months. There is a strangeness in the things around him . . . not just a strangeness between him and them, but a strangeness between them and themselves.

Beside the old-fashioned French doors that lead into the dining room, there is a lacquered Chinese-red table, a handsome eighteenth-century replica, upon which stands a tall solid ivory lamp with a tasseled gold shade, straight from the 1920's via a downtown auction house.

Hanging from the ceiling, there is a mobile composed of shaved steel fins. The rest of the room repeats this compulsive heterogeneity. The only object at rest is the massive color television set, which assimilates all things to its godlike tolerance of the tasteless, the vulgar and the anomalous.

Asa Bean peers about him briefly, thinking that—like Socrates with his wife, Xanthippe—if he can learn to be wise in a room such as this, he will have learned to be wise anywhere.

He sits and guzzles some more beer. Then he stares thoughtfully at the sky-blue ceiling, thinks of the art museum, and counts his trips there: one, two, three. By now, the guards are beginning to know him. He wonders if they know that he is carrying the loose-jointed, pearl-handled jackknife in his right pocket. Rapist of Masterpieces.

The phone rings, and Earlene calls out, "I'll get it."

Asa Bean, *c'est moi*. Same way.

13

Here I am.

Back between the dining room and kitchen, where the phone is kept, Earlene is saying, "Oh, hi, Madge!"

Then she says, "Yes. Oh, marvelous, Madge! Oh, marvelous! Okay. Sure, that's just fine. Good-by."

I hear the phone clopped back into place, and then the faint susurrus of Earlene's furry bedroom slippers on the bare floor between the dining room and living room. I look up, and she stops by the open French doors.

"That was Madge," she says. "You know, the local co-ordinator of FORCE."

"Sure, I remember. What's that acronym again?"

"FORCE."

"No, I mean, what do the letters stand for?"

"Oh. Feminine Opportunities for Revolutionary and Creative Effort."

"That's right. I remember."

"You'd like Madge," Earlene says. "She's quite a person. Not butchy at all; maybe bitchy, but not butchy. That's a joke she makes, but she's serious when she makes it."

" 'Not butchy, but bitchy,' " I repeat. "I kind of like it."

"Madge is really something special," Earlene says, curling down into a stuffed chair. "She's a medical technician in a hospital, but she could have been a doctor, if she'd been a man. I mean, it's *obvious*—considering her grades, and everything—that she has the ability. She's fantastically brilliant. I'd like you two to talk together."

I nod, and take a drink from my beer.

"I'd like to see the sparks fly," Earlene says. "I *know* you'd find areas of disagreement. I can hear the brains crashing together. I mean, you both have these fantastically analytical minds."

14

"You mean, she thinks like a man, is that it?"

"Now, that's a mean thing to say," Earlene cries.

"I was only fooling."

"Yes, but you probably meant it just the same."

"What's her last name?"

"Hunter. Madge Hunter."

"Is she married?"

"No, not now. She and her husband were divorced over a year ago. I just know you two would find each other fascinating. She's more help to people now than if she'd actually *become* a doctor."

Suddenly, the panel lights up. Sweet Earlene is thinking of mating the two of us. Her good friend, and admired leader of FORCE, and her only brother, who is obviously dying for lack of female comfort and attention, spelled "n–o–o–k–y."

But would Madge be the right one? I am intrigued, but a little leery. In fact, from the information I've gotten, I am distinctly ambivalent. I picture a quick stride across the floor, a comradely stare in the eye, a quick whiff of Dentyne gum, a flash of strong white teeth, a firm handshake, and then a loud, jackass bray.

Or she may be round and cuddly, have a lisp and walk with her toes turned in. God, you can never tell.

"Bring on your goddam jack whore!" a voice inside me cries, but the voice outside remains silent. That is the prudent voice, after all. The one that's killing me.

"Listen," Earlene says, soliciting my serious attention to a fabulous idea she has.

"I don't hear anything."

She draws in her breath quickly, and says, "Will you please *listen*? I have something I want to say to you. You could help us, you know."

"How's that?" I ask, once again wary. (The great bronzed buck in the thicket raises his muzzle and sniffs delicately at the traitorous breeze.)

"You could help us at FORCE, is what I mean. I've told Madge a few things about you, and she's interested. I mean, there's no reason—just because you're a man—you couldn't come and talk to us about the image of woman in Roman times. The ideal of the Roman matron . . . you know, the research you did one time for that article."

I brood for a moment, caught off guard. This is the only article of mine that Earlene has read, and I have had eleven published. But in all fairness, most have been published in periodicals that Earlene and her husband, Roy, haven't even heard of.

"Well?" Earlene says, her nose, ears, eyes and chin pointed with alertness.

"I don't know," I say.

"For someone who knows so much," she says, "you certainly never seem to know very much!"

This is as severe an irony as Earlene is capable of. One thing we know about our siblings: their exact capacities for irony. This is what childhood is all about. We extrapolate from there, and soon the whole world is sibling, and we play our ironies at one another like fugues of aggression and trickery.

"Listen," Earlene says, and I cock an ear, cup it with an eager hand, but she ignores this. "There's no reason you can't come and talk to us some evening. Your being a man is really irrelevant: it just so happens that you know more about women in Roman times than any of us, and the significance of Rome upon our civilization is hardly open to doubt. And I *know* you're sympathetic to our cause."

16

For an assertion, that last statement was strangely quizzical.

"I don't know," I say. "The ideal of the Roman matron was hardly the ideal of FORCE, it seems to me. Do you know all about *patria potestas*—the power of the father in Roman law? Hell, at one time a woman could be lent out, rather than given in marriage, so that the father retained all control over her . . . she couldn't hold property, and she couldn't . . ."

"That's exactly what I mean," Earlene says, with one of those brilliant silly reversals of thinking that leaves a man scratching his head and muttering. "You know," she said, "maybe that's where our problems all began!"

"Well, if you want to put it that way. . . ."

"Oh, Asa, you could help us so much, and all you do is give vague answers!"

"I don't know," I say. "But I *know* I don't know, so there's a certain Socratic wisdom in my stand."

"Oh, stand on your head!" Earlene says, and charges out of the room through the French doors, making the machine-shop mobile flash and flutter in the agitation of air.

I sit motionless for a moment, and then for some reason I start thinking of Durango.

Last week—my third week at the warehouse—Durango said, "Hey, Soy Bean, you married?"

"No," I said.

"What you do, rent a room?"

"Yes. I live with my sister."

"She married?" Durango said, with the villainy of pure artlessness.

"Yes, to a man named Roy Scobie," I said.

"What's he do?" Durango said.

"Sells real estate," I said.

17

"Good job," Durango said. "Must be rich. Shit!"

"He wants to be," I tell him.

Durango nods and looks thoughtful.

Durango, meditative on a warehouse field.

6

Who is this Asa M. Bean?

Let us refer to him as "X": ex-husband, of an intellectual wife with livid freckles, or brain spots, all over her skinny body, and a desire to know every single latest thing that is happening in the world of intellectual fashion; ex-student in the Ph.D. program at the University of Chicago, where he was writing a dissertation on the topic "Orphic Influences Upon the Epistemological Presuppositions of Gnosticism" for several months before his marriage dissolved beneath his feet, his wife left him, and he left the university (what a desperate diaspora was that!)—all this within two jim-dandy months of furiosity and alarums and broken sobs from the afore-mentioned confused and panicking wife.

Ex-husband, ex-student and ex-child, Asa Bean began to tend bar, and did so for eight months straight. Then he went to live with his sister, Earlene, with whom he now resides, working at the third job since the time of his death and rebirth (*sparagmos*).

Asa Bean, the Intellectual but Prurient Vandal, prevails, prepares, premeditates.

He is a man with a beard. He carries a pearl-handled jack-knife and visits art museums (one, particularly), listening to

18

the pictures. He is listening for the right one, and when the message comes through . . . zip, slit, slash.

Newspapers will report it that way, for they (newspapers) always think in plurals. Although they never say, RAPISTS ATTACK GIRL. Newspapers can get things right upon occasion.

Here is what Asa Bean does: He works in the produce section at the warehouse of The Great Atlantic and Pacific Tea Company. His shift is 5:00 A.M. to 1:30 P.M. daily, except for Mondays when he goes to work at 1:00 A.M.

He lives with his sister, Earlene, and her husband, Roy Scobie, at 1526 Marlborough Heights. He goes to work by bus and returns the same way. Roy Scobie is a young (thirty-one), ambitious real-estate salesman, who also happens to be, in theory, a Marxist ("Things are simply not ready yet"), and who worries about losing his hair, which is, in truth, falling out. Within another five years, Roy Scobie will look like a tonsured monk, but he will still wear long sad sideburns and a mustache, whether they've gone out of fashion or not. Some things abide.

Roy Scobie also reads sex manuals, and—as a real-estate man, but more importantly as A HUMAN BEING—he is obsessed with renting things. He likes real property. He says, "Some day, Marx will wipe all this out, but until that time we've got to go on and make it work." His eyes shine. He loves property, without realizing the fact.

"Which Marx," I ask him. "Harpo? Groucho?"

"Funny, Ace," Roy Scobie says. "Very, very, very funny."

He is a decent brother-in-law, when all is said and done, and takes good care of my nervous, dumb-ass sister, Earlene.

Earlene and Roy have a little baby daughter named Debra. Debra loves her Uncle Asa when he brings her things from broken crates at the warehouse. One day I brought her three ballpoint pens. Another time I brought her a can of Crisco. Another day I brought her two special bargain packs of Pride soap (bath size). All these from the grocery section where the fellows are generous and remember their hard-working colleagues in produce.

When I gave her the big can of Crisco, my little niece dropped it, just missing her toes.

"Asa," my sister said, "why do you give her such crazy things? It's too heavy for her to hold, for heaven's sake!"

I said, "But look at her. She likes it."

Indeed, Debra was sitting there on her little hunkers, trying to roll the heavy can of cooking oil.

"Honestly!" Earlene said.

Debra heard her voice and looked at her. Then she grinned, and turned her grin toward me. She looked malevolently wise at that instant.

"Debra," I said, "tell me: what is it all about? Come on, you can let your Uncle Asa in on the secret. Every time you pass by, I see you trailing strings of glory. Sometimes I almost step on them."

"Asa," Earlene said, "stop it, please. The poor child's too young for you to kid her like that."

"Then please explain that grin," I said.

7

The campaign is growing. The details accumulate, and the plan evolves. Things complicate themselves, like a vast tree, involuted with flowers, leaves and limbs growing out of a seed no larger than a dead button. Or bean.

Several months ago I saw an old movie on television (female), starring Walter Pidgeon as an English big-game hunter who decided that he would stalk the biggest and most dangerous animal of all, man; and not just *any* man, but the biggest and most dangerous man of that time, Adolf Hitler. So this great hunter arms himself with a high-powered rifle, equipped with a telescopic sight; and with great cunning and patience, he manages to get within rifle range of Hitler's balcony at Berchtesgaden. He raises his loaded rifle, focuses his telescopic sight—but at that instant is discovered and captured by the guards who are patrolling the area.

What the Nazis cannot understand in this situation is the omnipotence of fantasy that motivates the hunter. They cannot understand why it was *necessary that the gun be loaded if he did not intend to kill their Führer.* But of course, the British hunter insists that he would not have pulled the trigger.

It was a silly (female) movie (female), in a way; but after I watched it on television that night, with Earlene and Roy sitting there beside me (all of us drinking beer), and little Debra sleeping in her bed upstairs, I brooded about it. I thought about it when I was working as a delivery boy for pizzas (they told me to shave my beard or quit, so I quit). I have continued to think about it, at odd moments here and there, sometimes at the warehouse; and I have come to the conclusion that, no matter what the hunter said, there was a slight doubt in his mind, and that he might have, no matter how little he intended it at any prior time, squeezed the trigger at the critical moment. Becoming the Assassin.

The Anarchist and the Shawnee step forward and applaud.

It is said that Asa, King of Judah—famed in the Old Testament—was distinguished for his righteous fury against the powers of idolatry.

When the movie was over, Earlene said, "Let's turn the television off, honey."

She was talking to Roy, who had just stood up with the idea of going out to the kitchen and getting one last can of Miller's High Life. He was in his socks and skivvies, as usual. Not only is Roy a Marxist real-estate salesman ("Come on!" everybody says when I tell them this, but it's true; at least, he *thinks* he's a Marxist. I guess it's all a matter of interpretation), anyway, not only is he a Marxist real-estate salesman, who reads pornography and fears for his falling hair, but he is extremely hot-blooded, and when the rest of us (meaning Earlene, Debra and myself) are comfortably dressed for the house, with the thermostat set precisely at seventy-two degrees, nutty old Roy, my screwed-up brother-in-law, is sweltering and strips down to his socks, drawers and undershirt.

This evening, as I mentioned, Roy turns off the TV and walks out into the kitchen to get a can of beer, and Earlene asks me how I liked the movie.

"I am fascinated," I tell her.

"Honestly," Earlene says, "my heart was in my mouth."

Roy is returning with his beer, and he isn't going to let that go by.

"Far-fetched," he says, sitting down in his favorite chair.

"No, but it was so *interesting,*" Earlene cries out.

"How can it be interesting if it's far-fetched?" Roy argues.

She gives him a look and opens her mouth, but just gulps air and closes it again. If she'd been close enough, she would have slapped his knee and said, "Ooooh, you make me so *mad* sometimes!"

22

I am too busy thinking about the movie to speak just yet.

Earlene sees me and says, "What are you so busy thinking about? The movie?"

"Far-fetched," Roy said.

"Yes," I say emphatically.

"Far-fetched?" Roy asks, surprised that a momentary agreement between the two of us might be imminent.

"No, I was thinking about the movie," I explain.

"Oh," Roy says, frowning and examining the opening (female) in his can of Miller's High Life.

I decide, impulsively, to be candid: "As a matter of fact, I've been thinking for several years now of doing the same thing. Or practically the same thing."

"Hitler's dead," Roy announces with what he supposes is sarcasm. "I don't care what the *Police Gazette* has been saying for twenty-five years: Schicklgruber is dead, dead, dead, dead. Died with his pussy, old Eva Braun."

Earlene sniffs something interesting, and says, "Keep still a minute, hon. Asa's got something to say."

"Asa's got something to say!" Roy mimics. "Do we always have to play the same game? Listen to the visionary brother-in-law. The eccentric shaman, for Christ's sake. Asa's a real card, he is! Asa's wild." Favorite Roy Scobie joke.

"I want to hear what he's been thinking of doing," Earlene explains.

"I'll lay two to one it's more thinking than doing," Roy growls.

I get up and walk tiredly into the kitchen and get a beer for myself. Martyr whose suffering is mitigated by Miller's High Life. I buy most of the beer in the house, so I have tangible proprietary rights. As I pull a can out of the fridge, I keep thinking of how ridiculous it would be to tell Earlene and

23

Roy what I have been thinking. And yet, they are now the two human beings closest to me in all the world. And after all, you've got to talk to someone. Not only that, I am a little bit drunk from the beer.

When I return to the front room, I hear Roy say, "What he really needs, goddamit, is to get his ashes hauled about three times a night, and then he might calm down."

Earlene says, "Shhh," but it is too late. Anyway, I don't mind, because it's the simple goddam obvious truth. People can't believe this about me, but I have always been very shy where sex is concerned, and ever since a little blonde carhop named Ginny Troop got married, two months ago, I have been deprived of sex.

I go over to the chair and sit down.

"Well, go on," Roy says. "What is it the movie reminded you of?"

"Something you're thinking of *doing?*" Earlene asks intelligently.

"It's this fantasy," I explain. "For years, I've wanted to take a knife and go into an art museum and rip up a picture."

"What's that got to do with Hitler?" Roy asks, looking balder suddenly.

I take a long slow drink and say, "Next time I go into the museum, I'm going to take a knife with me. That's what. That knife is my loaded rifle. Get it?"

Earlene says, "Asa!" She thinks that somehow all of my gaucheries reflect upon her.

"That's a dumb thing to do," Roy says.

"It's a symbolic act," I tell him.

"Yeah, you resent accomplishment. You can't create anything yourself, so you go rip up a beautiful painting."

"That's not it at all," I say.

"That's a cruel thing to say, hon," Earlene tells him.

24

"Well, that may be," Roy says, "but people are going to think that's the reason."

"Destruction," I cry. "Destruction!"

"Asa!" Earlene exclaims. She really seems shocked.

"Vandalism," Roy says, shaking his head back and forth, "I can't even begin to understand." He points a finger at me, and jabs it back and forth in the air. "Theft is something I can understand. But not vandalism, for Christ's sake. You know what? Vandalism doesn't make any kind of sense. Robbery you might not approve of, but for Christ's sake, at least *somebody* is getting some good out of the thing you steal. Yourself, if nobody else."

"Asa, you shouldn't kid the way you do," Earlene says, getting up and starting to wind the clock over the mantel, with angry twists.

"I never kid," I tell them.

"Shit," Roy Scobie, my brother-in-law, says, staring at his can of beer. Then he shakes his head, smiling sadly.

"What's the matter, hon?" Earlene asks.

"I was just thinking about your brother," Roy says.

"What about him?"

Roy looks at me with an expression that is almost admiration. "Ace," he begins in that pontifical manner of his, "is the only person in the whole world . . . who would do this sort of thing."

"What sort of thing?" Earlene asks, sounding nervous. Sometimes she seems to be little more than a sensitive battlefield upon which Roy and I charge and counter-charge. It's really no wonder the poor girl has joined FORCE.

"Why, make *plans* to *vandalize* something!" Roy says. Then he laughs hard and long, but you can tell it is forced.

Earlene looks at me questioningly. "Is this true?" her look seems to ask.

25

"Vandalism," Roy says, starting to count his fingers the way Richard Nixon does, "is irresponsible, or it's nothing. I mean, vandals *don't make plans*. They act on impulse. They're stupid. They're not intellectuals, with an I.Q. of about four thousand, like the Old Ace over there."

"I guess if I were smarter I'd realize that what you say is true," I tell him.

Roy gets the irony, and snorts a brief laugh. But Earlene is still worried.

"Would you feel better," I say, "if we called it 'willful destruction,' instead of vandalism?"

"I don't really care what you call it," Roy says. "It's all a matter of semantics, so far as I'm concerned."

"Let's go to bed," Earlene says. "I think we're all too tired to argue."

Getting tired is something we can all agree on, so we go upstairs.

After I get in bed, I lie there thinking and suddenly I am astonished at the memory of all the secrets I have told. There was something reckless—even insane—in my divulging this enormous obsession I have. Except for this benign paradox: my speaking it out so casually to Earlene and Roy deprives it of significance. The mere fact that I talked about it transforms it into a kind of lie, for now they couldn't possibly understand the luminous enchantment the idea holds for me.

We are saved by the ironic and ambiguous.

All hail.

8

When I was a kid, I used to make lead soldiers. I would heat a gob of lead in a little flat-bottomed brass dipper, and watch it melt. That is exactly the way the sky looks now. The newspapers have predicted that we are going to have a blizzard late this afternoon and evening. There is a vague air of excitement somewhere in my stomach. I brood upon it. Other people must feel it too.

It is almost twenty minutes until quitting time, and we have gotten all our orders up, and there are no box cars to unload. Durango is lying on top of some potato sacks, apparently asleep. Tubbs is sitting on a stack of four pallets, dealing cards carefully along one wooden frame, and whistling tonelessly. Wilbur is in the office up front. Technically, he is our immediate boss, and might be in the front office on business, but we all know he is probably flirting with a redheaded secretary named Linda Thorpe.

Suddenly Durango turns over and looks at me. "Hey, Soy Bean," he says. "Pay Day, man."

"I noticed," I tell him.

"What you do'th all your money, Soy Bean?"

"I don't know. Spend it."

"Hell, I bet you save it," he says resentfully. Then, after a pause, he says, "Hey, Soy Bean, lemme ask you somethin. You Jewish?"

"Not that I've ever noticed," I say.

"Ain' that a Jewish name? Asa?"

"Yes, but so's John. And Thomas. Originally, anyway. My

father was a Methodist minister. He gave me a Biblical name."

"Reason I ask was," Durango frowns distinctly, "I was just curious. I mean, shit, didn make no damn difference to me you Jewish or not."

Tubbs changes the tune he's whistling, and Durango swings his legs around so that they're dangling off the load of pallets. Durango is a short, muscular Italian, with great brown, surprised-looking eyes and a nose like a shark fin. His beard remains a gun-metal blue, no matter how close he shaves. He always wears turtle-neck shirts and sweaters, even under his produce apron.

Durango stares into the distance, looking thoughtful. Finally, he says, "Let's you me drink a beer, Soy Bean."

I turn and look up at him.

"We ain' never drunk beer together, you 'n me," he says. "You ain' too good drink beer'th me, are you?"

"No," I say. I'm a little bit out of it, because I have been sitting there thinking about things. For a while I was thinking of broads: all shapes and sizes, in all positions. Wilbur's red-head up front (Linda Thorpe) was one of the *dramatis personae*. Sometimes one of the secretaries has to carry a message back into the warehouse. I keep thinking of rounding a corner on my bug, driving it with the forks about crotch high, and I jam into the redhead, who is on an errand of mercy, carrying a message to somebody in the grocery section that his grandmother has just died of cirrhosis of the liver.

Then I was thinking about my plan. I was trying to visualize the paintings in the art museum, and trying to get the plan of the building straight in my mind.

"Well?" Durango says, dropping to the cement from the stack of pallets.

"Sure," I say. "Didn't I say yes?"

28

"You didn say nothin," Durango says resentfully. "Look, Soy Bean, you don' have to drink beer'th me, you don' want to."

"I want to go," I say. "I just drift off now and then. Something wrong with my brain."

"Nothin wrong with your *brain,*" Durango says, correcting me. "Just your fuckin *mind* there's somethin wrong with, Man."

With that clarification, we let the matter rest, and wait until the clock (female) jumps to one-thirty, so we can ring (female) out and go for a glass (female) of beer.

9

It is cold as hell. A wind whips long crazy white veils of snow up the street and around the telephone poles. We are in Durango's metallic-green Mustang, waiting for the traffic light to change. The traffic light, showing red, bounces in the wind. The wind whirrs like a gigantic electric machine. The car quivers, and an icy draft sifts through the visor window at my side.

"Fifty below zero," Durango exclaims in characteristic Italian understatement. When I don't respond, he says, "*Sixty* below."

The light changes, and we glide out upon the street and head toward The Fifth Wheel, which is a bar about half a mile away on the highway.

By the time the heater is working, we are in the parking lot of The Fifth Wheel. Durango inches the Mustang forward, afraid for his new snow tires, until the wheels hit the cement diagonals. We step out into the wind and charge across the snow-flecked asphalt toward the projecting doorway (female) under a red-tiled gable. Mother (female) Goose (female).

Inside the bar, there are about a dozen people: two women (middle-aged, dowdy, defeated and uninteresting) and the rest men.

One of the waitresses is named Veronica. She is still fairly new at The Fifth Wheel, and this is only the third time I've seen her. Her face intrigues me. She reminds me a little of Dürer's "Portrait of a Girl in Lombard Dress." She has the same correct profile, the intelligent eyes and the cool expression. Her shoulders are a little round, and she has a prodigious ass that bobs like a carnival when she walks.

Durango always darts ahead, unless work is waiting. This is his life-style. Now, he spears himself into a dark booth near the corner, and yells for two bottles of Budweiser. "Nothin but the goddam best," he editorializes as I sit down across from him.

When I don't answer, Durango begins drumming his fingers on the table. He jerks the ashtray (female) over in front of him and starts reading it like a book. He turns it around a couple of times, and then drops it and starts whistling and snapping his fingers.

Durango is full of nervous energy. I am still trying to think about my plan.

Veronica bounces over slowly, and Durango leers up at her, with his mouth puckered for a kiss. Apparently this is a look that is supposed to knock Veronica dead, but she seems to be surviving all right. She places the bottles in front of us— plunk, plunk—each with a glass turned upside down over its neck (female, male).

Durango throws a dollar bill out on the table and says to her, "Whatsa matter, Veronica, don' you even pour your customers' beer?"

She gives him a tired, sour smile. "Sometimes," she says. Then she puts down his change and begins to climb away from the table, her ass bobbing all over like a load of balloons spilling out of a wagon.

"Jeeeessss—" Durango says, following her excursion back to the bar, "—uuuusssss!"

The juke box goes on, and Durango frowns until he recognizes the number, and approves. Then he hums along off-key, tapping a quarter from the change on the table. I can feel his breath on my hands, which are folded in front of me on the table.

We drink the first beer fast, and then slow down on the second one. Durango smokes a cigarette, then another. He talks about the new generator for his Mustang, the Philadelphia Eagles and a broad named Sylvia Stevens, who works in a bank. Durango claims he's getting into Sylvia's pants regularly.

But he's carrying the conversation. My mind keeps flying away like a flock of drunk pigeons. I am obsessed with this damned thing. Maybe Roy is right: maybe I am a little bit off. But *why not? Somebody* has to be off.

Silence.

Durango takes a long drag from his third beer, right from the bottle, and it plops loudly when he pulls it from his mouth. He is frowning, but no longer jerking all around and no longer tapping quarters and humming.

Then he says, "Soy Bean, what the hell you so fuckin quiet about?"

"Nothing to say, I guess."

"Bull shit. You got somethin on your mind is my guess."

"I need a piece of ass," I say, looking around at Veronica. "Shit, who don'?" The candour of his own utterance surprises Durango, and remembering what he has just said about getting into Sylvia Stevens' pants so frequently, you can see him draw up the reins and reconnoiter upon the spot. "I mean," he goes on "that's somethin a man *always* needs. Way I figure, you can't *get* enough pussy."

"Not only am I not getting enough," I say lugubriously, emptying my third beer, "I am not getting *any*. I only wish I were getting not enough."

Durango arrows a look into my misery. "Christ, man," he says, giving voice to one of the male's articles of faith, "it's all around. Pussy everywhere. Broads just achin to get laid. Just look all around you."

Both of us heard that, and we both automatically look up at Veronica. Then Durango looks back at me and says, "Hey, Soy Bean, you shy or somethin?" His face is darkly furrowed, troubled, uncomprehending.

"Sometimes," I say.

"You like old waddle-ass there?"

"Are you speaking of Veronica?" I ask, in the voice of an elderly judge.

"Sure. Veronica."

We both turn and look at her again. She is leaning her great abundance of warm buttock against the back of the bar. Her arms are crossed, and she is looking at the snowstorm through the side window, giving us her magnificent Dürer profile.

"I'll order another beer," I say.

Durango nods and says, "Good idea," as if he has just received something in code.

I wave my hand in the air, but Veronica isn't looking.

32

"Hey!" Durango yells, and Veronica turns and looks at us as if we are hiding underneath a parked car.

"Two more," I say, giving the victory sign.

When she brings them, I put the fingers up again and say, "That's 'V' for victory, right?"

Her eyes focus on mine. She senses something is up, and she is wary.

"Isn't it?" I say.

"I guess so," she agrees.

"It's also something else," I say. I'm beginning to panic. I'm going to sound ridiculous. I can't forget that I'm a loser. "It stands for Veronica."

"What does *that* mean?" she says.

"It means, help yourself to a beer on me, and then the composite sign for 'two-and-victory-and-Veronica' will become a composite sign for '*three*-and-victory-and-Veronica.'"

"What?"

Durango laughs and slaps the table with his palm. "Hell, don' listen to him," he says. "Soy Bean here just says he would like to buy you a beer."

Veronica looks doubtful a second, and then sort of laughs.

"Well, why didn't you say so," she says. "Is that your name? Soy Bean? That's crazy."

"That's why it's his name," Durango says.

She carefully removes thirty-five cents from the table and thanks me. Then she proceeds back to the bar.

"She likes that name," Durango says with the pride of a creator.

"Seemed to," I say.

"Christ," Durango says coming back to the immediate problem, "is that the way you go on the make?"

"That's my basic style. Why?"

33

"Why?" Durango raises his eyes to the ceiling and slaps the table with his open palm. "Why, he says! *Why!* Oh Jesus, you damn near scared her out of her *pants!*"

"That's just the way I want her," I say. "Out of her pants."

"Listen," Durango says, narrowing his eyes and leaning over close to me. "This isn't funny. You damn near scared her to death with all that tricky intellectual shit. Don' you know *nothin* about women? Christ, man, brains *scare* them. That's *right!* Scare the livin *shit* out of them."

Durango is getting passionate. The more intensely he feels, the lower he is whispering, as if the information he is giving me is dynamite, and no one else should hear.

"You'll scare her away forever, you try that 'victory' an' 'Veronica' shit on her again. She's probably over there right now, trying to figure out are you crazy or somethin."

I turn my head and see that she is standing precisely as before, with her profile to us.

"Don' look, don' look!" Durango hisses. "We don' want her to know you're interested. We don' want her to know we talking about her, man. Christ, don' you understand *nothin?*"

"A couple of things," I tell him.

Durango grabs my arm and says, "Look, you want in this broad's pants or not?"

For an instant I brood. I think of syphilis and gonorrhea. "Man lechers and lusts," I say, feeling vaguely as if I am quoting something, "throughout his days, but learns nothing and abides in loss and frustration."

"What's that supposed to mean?" Durango whispers. "Yes, goddamit, or no?"

"Yes," I say.

Durango nods and pats my arm. I had him worried there for a minute, but now I have come back in focus and there is something about me that he can understand.

34

"Jus' take it easy," he says. "An' do what I say."

I nod, and take another long drink. Then I turn my head once again, and am surprised to see Veronica staring at us, as if she could hear every word we have been saying.

Durango is my advocate. John Alden to my Miles Standish. Cyrano (he has the nose for it) to my Christian.

No, I am confusing (now an intransitive verb): the selves of Asa Bean confuse into a stream of verbiage . . . but isn't that what I want?

Durango will not plead for me. He will merely coach me. Be my manager. Durango, the manager of the fast-rising, fast, rising light heavyweight, or Light Heavyweight, Asa Bean.

Durango, *agent amateur,* assisting Asa Bean, *amator amateur*.

Durango, *advocatus fabuli*.

"Christ," Durango says, closing his eyes, "it scares the shit out of me when I think how near you come to screwin everythin up with that 'victory' shit!"

"I'll try to behave better in the future," I say.

Durango regards me silently for a second, and then he shakes his head. "You know somethin, Soy Bean? Sometimes you act like you about four years old. No shit."

10

I am lying in bed on my back, and I am half-asleep, dreaming of Veronica. She is sitting primly on a porch glider, ignoring me, and Durango is saying, "These things take time, Soy Bean. No decent broad's gone dive in bed with you right away. You got to finesse them a little bit, you know? Hell, Man, ain' you never had no experience with broads?"

There is a pounding on the door, and I wake up. It is little Debra, telling her Uncle Asa that breakfast is on the table.

The wheels start flying around in their circles. Two cherries and a plum. Ting-a-ling-a-ling. Coins spill out, and Asa M. Bean realizes that it is Sunday. It is cold outside. The window is so frozen it looks like aluminum foil. It is now three days since Asa Bean tried in vain, with the help of Durango, to finesse, or depant, the voluptuous, Düreresque Veronica.

Veronica has gone underground, like the ancient chthonic deities, and now she haunts Asa Bean's dreams. Veronica, the Succubus.

"What's he to Succuba, or Succuba to him?" Well may you ask.

The Anarchist, the Shawnee and the Assassin have, temporarily, given up. Exasperated, they have delved even deeper out of sight than Roy Scobie's bulletins, or Earlene Scobie's worries. Or the succulent succubus, Veronica.

Let me tell you, it requires something like courage to live with one's married sister, her husband, and their little Issue, Debra.

Which brings to mind that she is still pounding on the door, and calling out in dulcet but erumpent tones for her funny Uncle Asa to come down to breakfast.

The day threatens to be empty. I don't know Veronica's last name. Durango's approach would have been acutely embarrassing to me, *sans* the four bottles of Budweiser. Dutch courage, with the Dago Durango as *advocatus pudendi*.

Asa Bean is not only mad, he is sleepy. Furthermore, there is the odor of gently sizzling sausage upon the furnace-blown air. Little Debra has broken through, and now flings herself innocently upon the bed where her poisonously priapic uncle

36

lies filching at dream whores. (Oh, if the child only knew!) But perhaps, being woman (female) already, she is older than any male is likely to get, and takes these things in stride. She is pink and innocent and happy, and her Uncle Asa loves/pities/ adores her.

"Debra," I ask, "tell me the secret." I ask her so many silly questions, she never bothers to answer. She just flashes little preoccupied smiles at me, and rests content in my presence.

Downstairs, Earlene is calling. Roy is already warming up the television set for the Sunday World of Sports.

And I won't disappoint them. I shall descend in a moment. Perhaps I will even shave first, and, smelling of English Leather, join them to make cozy conversation over the jumbo pot of coffee.

Oh, Veronica, thy ass-mad Asa yearns for thee.

Descending the stairs, I have an explosively brilliant idea: I will cut Veronica and Durango in on my plan. They won't understand a thing. Veronica, however, will surely be moved by the boldness of the plan.

VERONICA THE VANDAL. DERANGED DURANGO. ASS-MAD ASA.

Fanfare of laughter from one good old-fashioned Anarchist, one Shawnee and one Assassin.

They have been there all the time, and of course Asa M. Bean was not fooled for an instant.

Asa knew.

11

It is interesting to ponder the history of one particular strand in the web of Asa Bean's fantasies.

Let us first consider him as an undergraduate. There is no greater testimony to Asa Bean's normality than his motivations at that time. Having read the existentialist canon, he became convinced that only the gratuitous act is free. And vandalism wears gratuitous clothing.

But then, being addicted to brilliance, he soon realized that being free isn't an absolute anything, let alone an absolute good. And furthermore, kindness is as eloquently gratuituous as vandalism. So he was forced to abandon such rubrics in the chapters of his thought as: "The Grand Act," "The Heroic Gesture" and (reflecting a period of ardent excursions into the later works of Henry James) "The Distinguished Thing."

Gone. All gone, serving him only as little voices from the past to mock him in what he had been.

But the fantast lived on, thriving and devouring his life with a truly Beansian energy.

It was Clement of Alexander who drove Asa Bean into the next phase, and soon the art galleries of Chicago were witness to the young student sitting and brooding at these graven images of an older religion of beauty. The old gods must go; ergo, the old images must go. (The Greeks, we are told, considered the early Christians atheists, because they had no graven images.)

But what religion would replace the old? Clement had Christianity, but Asa Bean's paternally imposed faith had evaporated with puberty and intellectual awakening. Asa's Methodist minister father, from whom he got the Biblical name, stirs in his bed of sighs at the old folk's home. Or is it conceivable that the ancient gods—like the acronymic Anarchist, Shawnee and Assassin of a later dispensation—were *only* driven underground, where they might continue their ontological productions more vitally than ever?

These are enduring puzzles, whose answers must involve

the entirety of Asa Bean's character and fate (which, of course, are one and the same thing).

In all this evolutionary flux, three elements remained unchanged: old paintings (preferably masterpieces), art museums (belonging to the public) and Asa Bean Himself. These are the three contrapuntal melodies that one hears throughout the fantasy-ridden years, always identifiable, always there.

Slashing, theft, burning, or some yet undiscovered outrage: these are the possibilities that hang like rich and sinister potential fruits, dangling above the head of our brooding Tantalus. Branches of the Tartarean Tree, bearing fruit and flowers.

The flowers are not unlike Veronica.

Often I come awake at night, prodded by a sudden tableau in the cinematic flow of my dreams. It is motionlessness that arrests; movement soothes us, and lets us sleep.

In this tableau, I am standing with the open knife before a painting. I am facing the painting, but I cannot identify it in any way, or see what it is. Prufrock procrastinating; Asa awed by the tangible imminence of such an act.

Who, if he understands contingencies, would dare to alter a single comma in the script of reality? Who, if he has a single spark of creative lust, does not dream of turning on the celestial showers for forty days and forty nights, and thus wash the old dispensation from the earth?

Today there was a letter from our father. Earlene cried, as she always does. Roy sat in a kitchen chair, drank a cup of coffee and steamed.

The letter was written by a Red Cross volunteer, and presumably the letter was dictated by our father (this is a manifestation of our faith that our father *really* says these things, which are penned for him by apostolic hospital volunteers).

In the letter, Father exhorted us to return to the old faith, and he quoted Scripture. Part of his epistolary litany is the quotation from Second Samuel, "For we must needs die, and are as water spilt on the ground, which cannot be gathered up again."

Our father broods upon his forthcoming death, and fears that we are afraid for him to die. Scarcely do we think of him, so cruelly are we immersed in the streams of the present. If I could get my ashes hauled, and if I could extirpate that glowing painting from my dreams and if I could pry that pearl-handled jackknife from my hand . . . then might I pity this fallen giant, who lies brooding upon the terror and confusion he will create by dying and leaving his two children to wander existentially lost beyond the walls of the paternal garden.

Also he said, "Miss not the discourse of the Elders."

He is a cantankerous old man, disputatious and presbytic, remote and zealous. Sometimes I cheer him on, as from a seat of perversity.

Always, his wild-ass letters drive Earlene to tears.

12

There is a sudden lull.

All the bugs are being used up front, in the grocery section. Out of my circumambient silence I can hear them droning away as they haul cartons of canned peaches, green beans and apple sauce stacked like building blocks upon the pallets they carry like alms upon their palpating, outstretched forks.

I am working with a giant hand-jack—a scarred and yellowed old veteran that has been standing in the repair room for years. Tubbs roars up on a bug, stops and stares at the jack. I continue pumping it up with the foot pedal, my hand on the release knob.

"Why you using that old thing, Soy Bean?"

"I just feel like it," I say. Tubbs shakes his head and roars away.

Wham. The legendary Soy Bean does it again. Using his muscles when it isn't necessary. Durango the classicist waits for a bug, refuses to budge until it's available. To walk is *infra dignitatem*.

But I need to think, and I often think best when my hands are busy. Do you hear that, Veronica? I am now loading banana crates on the pallet. I hear Durango whistling tonelessly in some unused part of the produce section. Up above, the slanted skylights are half covered with snow, and the enormous box cave we work in is now almost as dark as it is before dawn. The yellow lights in their dark green reflectors radiate their glow obediently, but still we shuffle about underneath, like troglodytes in the resonant and drafty gloom of the warehouse.

Suddenly, there is a roaring, and Durango whips around the corner. A Roman Emperor upon his chariot. Blue denim apron ripped at the waist (where it is faded and thin from hustling crates), so that a long string dangles behind. Durango wearing a violet turtle-neck sweater, a yellow pencil behind his ear. A load slip flapping in his hand.

"Soy Beeeeeeeeeen," he cries, as he turns down an aisle and disappears.

This is the man I have chosen.

With sideburns, I swear, he would look a little like a macrorhinous Che Guevara.

13

Another day. Brooding about the Plan. It seems more intensely inchoate than ever.

When I was a little boy, my mother would say, "But Asa, what is it you're trying to *do*?"

My father the Minister would say, "For God's sake, make up your mind and *do* it!"

Mummy asked, Daddy directed.

When I was in college, I told myself that neither M. nor D. understood the dimensions of the problem. They didn't know how big a balloon (sensibility) I was trying to tuck into how small a shed (definition, either of action or articulation—also, female).

Is it possible that a man might spend his whole life dedicated to an action he does not understand in the least? I am old enough to answer yes to this question, and mean it.

Is it possible that a man might spend his entire existence without really *having* a point to it? Yes. Or (Aristotle) is it possible that his life would be all *dynatos* (mockery) rather than *enteles* (haunting)? Yes, yes, yes.

But I am determined to fill out this action, by God, and it will be staged. The arena: an art museum. Stage properties: one or more handsome old oil paintings ("masterpieces"), plus one pearl-handled jackknife with loose blades. Actors: Asa Bean; Durango (?); Veronica (?). Major action: Uncertain (but more than a "happening," for God's sake!). Time: Uncertain, but within a few weeks (three weeks? four weeks? two days?)—goaded by an impulsiveness that Roy, quite correctly, says belongs to the true vandal. It is immoral for a vandal, *mutatis mutandis,* to premeditate.

Whatever one might say about it, this is a startling vision, a strange idea, an interesting idea. Veronica will dance around it in ecstasy when she hears. It will prove particularly exciting to women: it is illegal, it is bold, it is destructive, it is mad.

This is no nonentity that pursues thee, Oh Veronica! This is none other than Ass-mad Asa, the Unpredictable. Ravisher of masterpieces, tester of the cultural *pietàs* in this cloudy, compulsively relevant time.

Never forget, I cry, that freedom can only exist in the irrelevant. (Bean's Credo, framed in shining gold and illuminated by judiciously spaced lights in the third room of his cerebrum, down the right hallway.)

At no time will I be more free than at this apocalyptic moment.

Asa the Useless (free) among the sirens of purpose.

Veronica's excitement at the idea will surely prove overpowering. Her eyes will glaze over with love, and her thighs will loosen before the emblematic presence of Asa Bean's tyrannous satyriasis.

I will shake the pillars of the temple and eat courage from the head of the lion.

King Asa, the Righteous Iconoclast.

Blow, blast, stir the sauces of the heart.

Things fall apart. The center cannot hold.

Yes, but there are some who simply want to test "things," and do *not*—no matter how their actions are interpreted—wish to send the world spiraling into nothing, or worse, chaos.

Why *really* do I tease myself by going to the museum with my pocketknife?

It is an expression of irony, my basic stance toward myself, toward the world about me. It is irony that drives me from

43

women: the sudden vision of myself as I must look in the act of carnal intercourse, splitting a woman in half with long bestial surges.

"Not that women would ever object," I say to myself, but Oh God, that's not the point.

Where do you stand with reference to yourself? That is the question. I stand a little to the side and above myself, and watch the poor dumb animal thrash through his quotidian delusions and angers and confusions as if I had him on a leash.

And in the same spirit I send myself skipping brainlessly into the art museum, wondering if I will commit the shockingly gratuitous act, and fearing I will and fearing I won't—split like the female passivity by the arrogant rutting mind that motivates and torments me.

But that isn't right, either. For how could I ever let my words turn like mad dogs back upon their master, Mind?

Irony, irony, irony.

Now I am standing on the corner, waiting for the bus to veer over to the curb on its great gummy wheels and accept my presence. Durango called in sick today. Tubbs had a hangover. Two men from the grocery department came back and helped us for a couple of hours. There's a boxcar load of potatoes that will have to wait for tomorrow, however, before we can unload it. If Durango calls in sick again tomorrow we'll get overtime. Not that Asa Bean craves it.

I was going to go to The Fifth Wheel to see Veronica, but it's too cold to walk, the bus doesn't go that way, and I am tired as hell for some reason.

I will go home and dream of her, to an obbligato of little Debra's footsteps about the house.

I can sleep anywhere, anytime. It is a marvelous gift.

Of course I would rather sleep with Veronica, anytime. What a gift *that* would be!

Mama Bus comes up and tiredly wheezes her doors open. I enter, drop my token in the little glass case (also female—a chest within a chest within a chest) ordained for the reception of tokens, weave my way back to an empty seat (female) and place myself carefully beside a girl of about twenty, who is chewing gum and wearing glasses. Otherwise, not bad though: perky tits and snug little thighs pressed together, faintly bronzed by panty hose . . . and the whole confection designed by God, with the help of a multitude of anonymous New York fashion fairies (crypto-female), simply to drive Asa Bean mad.

Look, but don't touch.

I see the signs all around me. They flash on and off in neon. Transistor radios play it to the tune of a well-known tango. *Vide, sed non tangere.*

Asa Bean, sitting in a brief snit of nisus.

But Asa's brains relieve him, for he knows that all senses are mere translations of touch. Therefore, he lowers his face, pretending to ponder, with his hand clasping his forehead; and the rascal stares at her milky thighs, snug together and faintly chocolated by panty hose that connect her tiny toes with the glutei maximus, medius and minimus, and the sweet little bird nest (bird of paradise) ensconced within.

The girl snaps her gum, wafting a brief hint of Spearmint into the bus's lambent drafts. Asa Bean's velleities snap like overtested, rotted threads, and his mind whirls into rockets, bursting fires, muted flowering plosions in the night of longing, shaking like great 4th of July streams of salt underneath the stars; and knowing that, ultimately, sight and touch are one and the same (*sub specie aeternitatis*), Asa Bean drinks

45

the girl's beauty dry, and no one on the whole bus is aware of the fantastic rape.

Ravished, ravishing.

14

Last night it warmed up a little and snowed again. Uncle Asa took Debra out in the back yard where, amid great frolic, they gathered snow for snow ice cream. Earlene made it the way our mother used to do, with lots of sugar and vanilla. Then we all sat around a cozy fire (dumb old Roy in his skivvies, as usual) and ate the ice cream, and talked. Earlene told stories about when the two of us were kids. To hear Earlene tell it, I certainly was a corker. A card. A whimsical youth. A terror. An enigma.

Anyway, after little Debra went to bed, Earlene had a crying spell. She said it was all the memories of our childhood and of poor Mum and Daddy. Daddy, the retired Methodist minister, is paralyzed, living the life of a vegetable in an old folk's home in Illinois; Mum is dead.

Roy was silent, uncommunicative. I think he considered me somehow responsible for Earlene's outbreak. God knows, the poor girl is nervous and rattle-headed, but I hardly think I'm the reason. Every other week I make a formal offer to leave the House of the Scobies, but Roy gets a quick flick of panic in his eyes and says, "No need to rush off, Ace. I mean, hell, for Christ's sake."

We danced this same dance, strophe and antistrophe, last evening, and decided that I was right where I belonged.

"When you get married again," Roy said, "then you'll naturally want to shove off. But hell, until that time . . ."

I know what he's thinking of: all the cases of Miller's High Life I put in the fridge, plus the room and board I pay. At the rate I'm going, I'll be putting little Debra through college. Not to mention all the heavy beer fat I'm putting on Roy.

Right before I went to bed, Earlene went out to the kitchen, and Roy mentioned the Plan. "You still thinking of those old paintings?" he said.

"The thought," I said, "occupies me day and night."

"Never mind the bull shit! I just asked a simple question."

"Well, I'm still thinking of it, Roy."

Roy just shook his head. The television was on. It was the Johnny Carson Show, and Johnny was opening some newly invented toys, and making wry comments about them, and making elf faces at three-quarters view, while the audience laughed.

"You better give it a lot of thought," Roy said. "That's all I can say."

But of course, whenever someone says, "That's all I can say," you know that more is coming. And it was this way with Roy.

"I've got only one request to make of you, Ace," he said. (This, too, is always a lie.)

"What's that?"

"Well, Asa, if you decide to go through with this crazy thing, I'm going to ask you to think of your sister and niece."

"You mean Debra?" I asked.

"Now don't be so goddam smart. I'm trying to be serious. Of course I mean Debra. And your sister, Earlene, in case you've forgotten her name."

47

"All right," I said.

"All right," Roy said, "what I want you to do is to leave if and when you do this crazy thing with those paintings. Because if they trace you, I don't want them tracing you to 1526 Marlborough Heights."

"You mean here," I said.

"Will you for Christ's sweet sake shut up, you dumb shit?" Roy cried.

"I could leave now, if you really want me to," I said.

"Oh, Christ, let's not go through all *that* again. I'm talking about if you *do* this crazy thing. I'm only thinking of Earlene and the baby, for God's sake! What I'm hoping is, you'll get some sense in that head of yours before you do anything rash."

Earlene returned from the kitchen, and I could see that her eyes were still red and swollen. "What's wrong now?" she asked, spiraling down into a big stuffed chair.

"We're just talking, hon," Roy said, glaring at me. "Nothing wrong at all."

"No," I said. "Everything's okay."

Roy hadn't let his gaze jar a centimeter from my face. It was as if he were trying to communicate something to me by telepathy. But he wasn't; he was just winding up to speak.

"Asa," he said, shaking his head back and forth with the wonder of it all, but still not moving that stare, "do you know what you need?"

"Love and understanding?" I asked.

"No, what you need is . . ."

"Money?"

Earlene said, "Asa, can't you see that Roy is trying to tell you something?"

"All right," I said. "What is it?"

"You, you goddam screwed-up misfit, need to get laid. That's l–a–i–d. You need to get some hot bitch you can screw

48

about every half hour, and take some of that piss and vinegar out of you. You need a good, warm-ass woman to bring you down to size. You work hard enough at the warehouse: I'll give you credit for that, but it isn't normal and it isn't healthy for a thirty-year-old man with your energy to go without good pussy day after day. It isn't *healthy* for you not to get your ashes hauled and your temperature simmered down. You know what I think? I think it's driving you crazy. Men have been known to go *crazy* from prolonged sexual abstinence!"

When it was evident he had finished, Earlene stirred on her chair, and said, "Roy, I wish you wouldn't talk that way."

"Well, it's the truth," Roy said.

"Maybe so, but I don't think you should talk that way."

I didn't say anything. In spite of his fouled-up physiology and his tangled metaphors, Roy had come awfully close to speaking the truth. I was ready to agree with him. But how could I tell him that I was shy and ineffectual with regard to sex?

He would have said, "Hell, you were *married* once, weren't you?"

How would I have fielded that one? It was a long and complicated story about how my first wife (I trust there will soon be another; do you hear, Veronica?) and I got together. It was as much her doing as mine, and more the doing of accident than of either participant.

I sometimes wonder how intelligent people ever manage to reproduce themselves, possessed—as they inevitably are—by a sense of irony. Now take Durango . . . irony has never pitched its tent upon that fellow's intellectual domains, and yet even Durango is not entirely free of bashfulness. Which is *near* to irony.

15

The Fifth Wheel is warm and steamy. Veronica's face is red, and a fuzzy curl gestures like a beckoning little finger, stuck to the perspiring skin on her left temple.

Durango and I are sitting in the same booth. We humans, I am thinking, repeat old gestures and old patterns, and return to familiar places, in order that we may have memories. Clearly, my sinister counter-faith is that some of these memories need to be blocked off.

I have just adumbrated the Plan to Durango. His response is curiously shielded and dignified. I thought that my words would evoke some latent Sicilian bandit from the reservoirs of Durango's blood. I was looking for some knife-glint of interest, or of recognition, even, in Durango's heavy brooding eyes.

When I have finished this phase of the communication, I pour some more Budweiser into my glass.

Durango frowns and says, "Soy Bean, somethin I been wantin to ask you. How come you workin in a goddam lousy fuckin warehouse?"

"It's not so bad," I say.

"Hell no, it ain' *bad*," Durango says, contradicting all the rhetoric he had just released, "but the question is, how come you *workin* there?"

The question is a critical one, calling for some decisive action—like equivocation.

"Well," I say, rubbing my chin with my hand and closing one eye (Long John Silver, morally tarnished, contemplates a trick he might play on innocent Jim Hawkins).

"Well, what?" Durango says.

"Well, that's a pretty good question."

"Hell, I knew that when I asked it."

"*Why* did you ask it?"

Durango frowns even harder. He's working at the frown. He twirls his glass in both hands and meditates. Finally he says, "Soy Bean, there's somethin wrong with a man workin in a warehouse when he's got a college education, that's all I got to say."

"Everybody's got to work somewhere."

"Sure, but in a *warehouse*? Throwin around them fuckin *lettuce* crates? Throwin around fuckin hundred-pound sacks of *potatoes*?"

"What," I ask, "does that have to do with my Plan?"

"I'm gettin to that," Durango says. "Fact is, Soy Bean, I think you okay. I mean, shit, Man, I'm your friend. You know? No shit: your friend. But the fact is, Man, you got a screw loose somewhere. I mean, first you got a college education, you come work in the fuckin warehouse. Then you figure up some screwy goddam plan like"—Durango's voice changes, gets deeper and hoarser, his eyebrows go up in his forehead, and he waves a hand in the air, released by a sudden charge of adrenalin and rhetoric—" 'I'm gone go in this here art museum and give these here masterpieces the treatment, because they grand to us, or the act got two of us. . . .' "

"The word's 'gratuitous,' " I say.

"I don' give a shit what the word is," Durango says, "I *still* don' know what in the hell you *talkin* about."

The admission makes us both despondent, and we sip our Budweiser. I glance toward the bar, and see Veronica leaning over in our direction. She's getting some bottles out of the waist-high, or pussy-high, cooler. The top of her head is pointing at me. If she blew her top, I'd be right in the line of fire. She has a part right down the middle of her head, showing naked white scalp—about a quarter-inch strip. For all her flesh, she has little-boned shoulders. I could grab each one and work them around inside the flesh, like two universal joints, and her eyes would glaze over, and she'd say, "Soy Bean, give it to me!"

"I mean, shit," Durango says, "you want to *steal* a fuckin painting, and you got some place to *sell* the goddam thing, well maybe I understand what the fuck you *talkin* about, but this thing about goin up there in the goddam gallery and cuttin a painting *up,* as an act of *communication,* for God's sake . . . I mean, that don' make no sense to me at all, Soy Bean. Me, I rather take a good long nap than do somethin stupid like that."

Clearly, Roy and Durango are brothers under the skin. But what did I expect? Did I *want* Durango to understand? How would he have communicated his understanding? By not asking the obvious questions, and by not saying he *didn't* understand?

Careful, Asa Bean. That sounds a little like bull shit.

16

Never mind about Durango. Never mind about the Plan. Both can wait.

I have a date with Veronica!

When Durango found out about it, he slapped me on the back and congratulated me as if I had just sired a son who would grow up to be rich, tough and smart, in that order of precedence.

At nine o'clock, we all went to a little lunchroom called Harvey's, where we usually eat. It's still cold and dark. Durango, Tubbs, Wilbur and I are seated in a booth. Our waitress is named Melba, and she is built like a big lumpy lightbulb, or an enormous sack of pumpkins. She is the nearest thing in human guise I have seen to that primitive fertility goddess, the Willendorf Venus. She wears too much lipstick, and her long hair is turned under at the tips, so that her face reminds me a little of Deanna Durbin reflected in a funhouse mirror.

Melba slaps coffee down, one, two, three, four, in front of us without waiting to ask. She knows us better than she knows her own knees. We order (she writes the orders a little ahead of us), and then she whips back to the counter, to hang the order on the serving wheel behind.

"Hey, Soy Bean," Durango says, "old Melba there makes Veronica look like Fred Astaire, don' she?"

Durango brays a laugh, and Tubbs and Wilbur grin, stirring their coffee.

"Speaking of whom," I say, "I might mention that I have a date with her."

"Veronica?" Durango cries, astonished.

"Well, certainly not Melba. And certainly not Fred Astaire."

"Hey, Man, great. When this happen?"

"Yesterday. I stopped in The Fifth Wheel and went up to her without ordering anything and asked her what time she got off work today."

"You got a date with her *today?*" Durango said. I think he is a little disappointed that I didn't let him engineer the whole thing.

"She said that she would be off work today at five o'clock, when all the evening help comes in, and she would be pleased to go out with me."

"Where you takin her?" Tubbs asks.

"Out to dinner," I say. "I'm not sure where."

"Better pick a place yourself," Durango advises. Durango looks serious. "She might spend all your money. Thing is, don' spend no more money on them you can help until you get in their pants. Then it's okay."

We all contemplate this worldly advice for a while, and then Melba returns with a dish of prunes for Wilbur, which he eats every morning.

Veronica is so much in our minds at the moment that we neglect to kid Wilbur about the prunes, and he is forced to eat them unmolested and in silence.

Durango says, "Tell you what. To show you my heart's in the right place, I'll lend you my car. You don' wanna take no fuckin goddam cab."

"No, that's okay," I tell him.

Durango shakes his right hand in the air, fingers spread. "Okay, hell! Look, I *want* you to take the car. Okay? I'll ride home with Tubbs."

"Okay," I tell him. "And thanks."

17

The snow is turning dark, rotting like great scatterings of Paleozoic teeth along the gutters. And yet it is not melting. The temperature this morning was nineteen degrees. It will rise to thirty; no more.

Life in the boneyard will continue unchanged for a while. The weather will turn colder, but there is no immediate likelihood of additional snow.

I ease Durango's Mustang into a parking space between two other cars. The parking lot is crowded, and I figure business is good.

As I walk across the parking lot, toward the gabled entrance, my throat is thick from *globus hystericus*. When I try to speak to Veronica, I will choke up and all she'll be able to hear is a kind of growling, like the starter of a car when the battery is tired.

That's it: I want her to crank me, and make my engines purr.

God, I've got to watch the metaphors. Maybe Durango is right. On the other hand, maybe Veronica has an I.Q. of 172, (virtually commensurate with, or approaching, thine, Oh Asa!), and reads Aeschylus in the original Greek. Maybe she speaks Latin to her cat and works advanced problems in mathematics, devoting her leisure hours to Boolean algebra and imaginary numbers.

Careful, Asa. She probably doesn't even have a cat. Where is your reality principle, for Christ's sake?

I open the door, and step inside, leaving the Anarchist, the Shawnee and the Assassin out in the cold. I stand there reconnoitering an instant, and remove my ski cap.

I walk up to the night manager, whose name is Craig Todhunter. He is a fat man with freckles and red hair. I like to fantasize about what happens when Craig and Veronica have to pass each other behind the counter, rubbing their nether regions together. Oh to be as fat as Craig Todhunter, working behind a counter with the plethorapygian Veronica!

Craig looks up when I approach, and says, "She left a note for you. She had to go home early."

He hands me a tidy little envelope with my name on it. The handwriting is small and even. Veronica is an orderly person, and the sight of the handwriting swells my heart with some unidentifiable emotion.

I sit on the nearest bar stool, and read the note that says:

I'm terribly sorry, but my father had a bad fall today, and I have to go home and take care of him.

Sincerely,
Veronica

P.S. I won't be able to go out to dinner with you tonight. I hope you will understand.

V.

"She got a phone call and had to leave in a hurry," Craig Todhunter says, leaning over the bar toward me. He's wiping his hands on something underneath the bar. He whispers: "I think her father is off the wagon again. Son of a bitch is really bad on the sauce. When he falls off the wagon, you can hear it for miles around."

Craig agitates his fat body, and glancing at his face I realize that he is laughing. "You want a Budweiser?" he asks, seeing that I am sitting down.

"Sure," I tell him. "I guess so."

I might as well.

After I finish my first Budweiser, I buy another, and take it over to a booth and sit down. Through the venetian blinds at my side, I can see through the steamed window, and in the darkness I can make out Durango's Mustang, settled quietly and obediently between two station wagons.

I drink one more Budweiser, then have a cheeseburger with onions, and a cup of coffee.

Having finished eating and drinking, I put on my hat and

56

coat, go out and get in the Mustang, and drive it back to 1526 Marlborough Heights.

I can drive the Mustang over to Durango's tomorrow morning, and then he can take me to work in it.

Poor Durango, his faith in me will be shattered.

Poor Veronica, for whether she has lied or told the truth, there is the possibility of pain and suffering and muddle-headedness there.

Poor Anarchist, Shawnee and Assassin. They are imprisoned in a woefully inept man. Who knows? Perhaps some day, intelligence will be as useless and irrelevant as any other vestigial organ.

"You are victimized by your own I.Q.!" Earlene once shouted at me, when I had just out-tricked her in an argument. "You can't see a thing in the real world; your intelligence keeps getting in the *way!* You can't even look at a woman without glossing a thousand texts from Aristophanes to Chaucer. You're horribly, brilliantly *insane,* that's what you are!"

Poor Earlene: that was her most eloquent, most oxymoronic moment.

But then, poor all–of–us!

Poor Ace O'Bean, the slain Celtic hero. He is a monster, a primitive mollusk, a bristling, spiny atavism upon the shores of desuetude, an acanthopterygian monk, basking in the fury of a celestial vision. He is a brontosaurus, mooing and thundering for a worthy mate. He is a throw-back, a vestige, a—forgive me (forgive yourself!)—Has-Bean.

Maybe the world's right, and an excessive I.Q. only makes one ridiculous.

18

"That still doesn't mean she stood you up," Roy says. His voice is scholarly, judicious, well-informed in such arcane matters.

"No. She was *probably* telling the truth," I say.

It is evening. I am standing at the counter beside the sink, making a salami, dagano cheese (as smooth, soft and cool as a virgin's thigh), sliced tomato, hot pepper, lettuce and onion sandwich on toasted whole-wheat bread. Roy is standing behind me, in his underwear, drinking a Miller's High Life from the can. Earlene is attending the monthly meeting of FORCE. When he told me where she had gone, Roy said, "Yes, the girls are having their monthlies."

"I wouldn't take it too lightly," I said.

"You don't take *anything* too lightly," Roy said, "except things that are serious."

Now we are getting dinner for ourselves, because Earlene hasn't returned yet. Debra is staying with the woman next door, and her four children. The woman is also pregnant.

When I finish making my sandwich and take it, along with a can of Miller's, into the front room, Roy follows me.

I turn on the television, and Roy says, "Listen, Ace, I got to talk to you."

I turn the television off, and say, "Sure. What is it? Want me to leave again?"

Roy makes a face and says, "Will you be serious, for Christ's sake?"

I tell him I will and Roy settles in a chair, leans forward

with his elbows on his knees and begins to frown. Finally, he says, "You really think I'm a dope, don't you, Ace?"

That surprises me, and I tell him that this isn't the case at all, and I furthermore tell him that I am surprised at the very thought.

He looks at me and nods, as if that is a most reasonable answer. Then he bites his lip.

"Well," Roy says, "that isn't the main point anyway. It was just a passing thought, although it's a thought that passes pretty frequently."

I start to say something, but he waves his hand to dismiss any protest I might make. Obviously, this is *not* the thing he wants to talk about.

"What the problem is," he says, shaking his head and focusing his eyes on the floor between his feet, "is this goddam feminist kick Earlene is on. You know, I don't want to say anything to her about it, because I'd hurt her feelings. And not only that . . . hell, I want Earlene to participate in something meaningful. I mean, shit, Ace, there's a lot *to* the gripes these broads have. When Earlene shows me their literature, and everything, I mean, I'm really sympathetic. Karl Marx knew the score on this thing. A lot of what they say makes sense. You know, that bit about women being chattel, and male chauvinism. The other day she sprang one on me that strikes me as being damned good: 'The masochism imposed upon women.' Isn't that great? And a lot of truth to it, too. Son of a bitch!"

He pauses and takes another long drink of beer. There is a hole in one of his wool socks, and for some reason this strikes me as rather strange and pathetic. Old Roy, the balding hot-blooded Marxist realtor and Master of Curiosa, doesn't have it all milk and honey, being married to Earlene.

He clears his throat and continues, "But, hell, I don't

59

know. You've met this Madge Hunter broad she's always talking about, haven't you?"

I shake my head no, and Roy says, "You haven't?" Then he whistles, and shakes his head wonderingly. "Let me tell you something, Ace, you've got a treat in store for you. Yes sir, a treat in store. Anyway, I think this broad is most of the trouble. She's really potent medicine, Ace. No shit. When she gets wound up, every goddam broad in hearing range starts to nod and get indignant over things they never even noticed before. Madge Hunter has charisma. And she's smart as hell, too."

He stopped suddenly, as if he heard a noise. "You know something? These women are planning some kind of demonstration. Something big, a disruption, or some goddam thing. I honestly don't think Earlene herself knows what it is yet, even though she's on the local Board of Directors now. It's some big secret, whatever it is. But of course, I don't want to press her too hard. You know how it is."

"Sure," I say. I am beginning to wonder what the point of all this is; but Roy seems to detect my suspense.

"This is where you come in," he says, giving me a grim, all-business look.

"Where?"

"Right here. I want to tell you something that you know very well: Earlene thinks you're really something special. I mean, she would listen to *you* in a way that she wouldn't listen to a *husband,* if you know what I mean. Now my point is, if *you* were to talk to her about FORCE, and some of the ideas behind it, she might simmer down a little bit. I don't like to see Earlene get this upset, Ace. That's the truth. And then there's Debra to think of. You know, all this feminist shit isn't about to do a little girl that age any good."

"What do you want me to say to her?"

60

"Well, hell, I don't want to presume to tell you what to say. That'd be like an altar boy giving advice to the Pope. But I figure *anything* to make her simmer down a little bit. Not that Earlene would ever do anything to me. I mean, hell, I know our marriage is perfectly sound, and perfectly happy. But I'm thinking if maybe she didn't look up to this Madge Hunter broad so much, and if she didn't brood so goddam much over what she's *deprived* of, being a woman, instead of what she's *entitled* to, being a woman. . . ."

" 'Sir, the law cannot afford to give more power to a woman; nature has given her far too much already.' I'm quoting somebody, but I don't know who. Dr. Johnson, I think."

"That's good," Roy says appreciatively. "That's very goddam good."

"Especially if you don't believe it too much," I say. "Like all epigrams."

There is a sudden humming sound outside, and Roy and I turn in its direction. Earlene has just driven the car into the driveway, and is about to maneuver it into the garage. But then the humming stops, and it is replaced by the sound of two doors slamming, and then women talking.

"Good God," Roy says, jumping to his feet, "she's bringing somebody in with her."

He darts out to the kitchen just as Earlene comes in with another woman. Earlene has already gotten Debra from next door. The child is half-asleep, and blinking resentfully out upon the world of light. Good child. Earlene and the other woman are both smiling, and looking very confident. Earlene removes her coat, staring at me as she does so. The other woman is removing her coat, too. She also is staring at me. Their actions are a little like those of a tag team of female wrestlers. Neither speaks, but both are looking vital and ruddy from the cold.

61

Earlene finally says, "Asa, I want you to meet my very good friend, Madge Hunter. Madge, this is my brother you've heard so much about: the family genius."

Madge Hunter is fairly tall, fairly well-built and fairly fair. She wears glasses with sequined rims, and her hair is parted exactly in the middle, the way Veronica wears hers. Her eyebrows are a little thick for a lady, and her shoulders are a little broad; but she is distinctly feminine, and I am kind of interested already.

She says, "How do you do, Asa," and steps forward, holding out her hand. I clasp the hand, and we shake it up and down several times. Warmly. (In fantasy, I throw her back on the sofa and have her five or six times, while Earlene evaporates somewhere and smokes a cigarette.)

"Where's Roy?" Earlene asks.

"He's in the kitchen," I say. "You surprised him. *In flagrante delicto scivendi.*"

"Madge knows Latin," Earlene says, with a knowing grin on her face. Does she think I'm faking and will now be *exposed?*

"Really?" I ask.

Madge laughed. "I got the *'In flagrante delicto,'*" she says, "but I didn't quite get the last word."

"Just a little neologism," I say. "Meaning, wearing his skivvies."

"Oh of course," Madge says, turning with her eyes sparkling. "Earlene told me what to expect. I'm not bothered by such things."

"What things?" I ask, but Earlene obviates an answer by trotting out of the room with Debra, whom she has kept snuggled against her maternal breast all this time. We hear her go upstairs and deposit the child in her bed, and then come straight back (Debra being a wise and talented sleeper,

62

with none of the tantrums associated with beddy time), and return to the front room, saying, "Everything okay?"

"Just fine," Madge says. "Just relax and do what you have to do. We're doing fine."

Earlene flashes a brief smile at me, and then departs once more, this time headed for the kitchen. We can hear her quite clearly say, "Roy, for heaven's sake, come on out! Don't be primitive. Madge is the last person in the world to be embarrassed by a man in underwear. I told her about your habits, and she thinks it's perfectly all right. Perfectly natural. Roy, for heaven's sake, don't be such a *moron!*"

All this time, we don't hear any answer at all, and for an instant I think maybe Roy has bailed out the kitchen window, into the nasturtium bed outside, but then we can hear whispering (Roy) and loud, cheerful, let's–be–honest–and–natural talk (Earlene).

Madge walks around the room, looking at the paintings and laughing silently. She seems to be pantomiming the relaxed, aggressive male, walking onto an unused stage-setting. She is obviously picking up on everything that is being said in the kitchen, and equally obviously aware of my watching her buttocks (turned loose to graze in the meadows of my approval) as she tours the room. For all the eeriness of the situation, however, I cannot for the life of me see anything unfeminine about old Madge. In fact, I am applauding her at every step. She might have a convert. With a little luck, she might show enough aggressiveness to rape me, and relieve me from the tyranny of that brutish sting that poisons my fantasies from morning till dusk.

"Here he is," Earlene says, escorting a vaguely beaming Roy (embarrassed) in from the kitchen.

"Hello, Madge," he says. "You kind of surprised me. I wasn't expecting Earlene to bring anybody in with her."

Madge laughs good-naturedly and says, "Sure, I understand. But we're friends, and friends don't have to conceal things."

I wonder what she means by that. And as if to demonstrate (ambiguously) an answer, Madge steps forward again (like a fencer attacking) and shakes Roy's reluctant hand. I notice, however, that her glance does not stray downward toward Roy's more vulnerable parts. Everything is above board. On the up and up.

"Well," Earlene says, "sit down, Madge, and I'll get us all a beer or something."

Madge says, "Oh, I feel like standing. A beer would be nice, though."

"We keep them cold," I say fatuously.

She turns her bright beam toward me and says, "Hmmm?"

"I said, 'We keep our beer cold.' Miller's High Life."

"Oh," she says, sliding her glance past Roy (still standing like a clod), and then back to the damned pictures. I suddenly pick up on this, and realize she is looking at my favorite—one I gave Roy and Earlene for Christmas a few years ago—a print of Cranach's "St. Jerome in His Study."

Madge is gazing at it and itemizing Jerome's companions in the study, in a voice hardly above a whisper: "Pheasants, lion, dog and books."

"What more does a man need?" I ask.

She beams at me again, and says, "Woman."

That almost breaks me apart, and all I can do is gape foolishly, my mind spiraling about the room like a released balloon.

Earlene returns with four beers and four sparkling clean glasses, on a tray. Her mouth is all pursed up, and I realize she's all excited about getting old Asa and Madge together. I don't know whether it's the mating instinct, or the thrill of being a spectator of the clash of ideas and/or intellects. Maybe both, or all three.

"Well," Earlene says, when she curls down in the big chair (Madge is still standing, holding her can of beer—having refused the glass—and still attending to the Cranach print of St. Jerome).

"Madge and I were talking all the way home," Earlene says, "about the whole sex thing between men and women. And how it's so unfair. Unfair to *both* sexes. Naturally shy men, for example, are at a terrible disadvantage, simply because our stupid conventions frown on women being aggressive."

I hear the clap of a cigarette lighter, and see Madge lighting up. Roy is staring at me like an ox that has just been hit by the big club. I can't decode his look at all: it might be, "Speak of the devil! (Madge)" or it might be "Christ, where do we go from here, Asa?"

But I'm not about to side with him at this juncture. I know whose side *I'm* on. At least at the moment.

"Precisely," Madge says, without turning away from dumb old St. Jerome.

I don't know what the "precisely" is supposed to fit, but I'm only half listening, anyway. I don't feel like arguing. The expression "sex thing" has clotted the flow of my mind. After the betrayal of Veronica (yes, betrayal), I am grasping at straws. Or, more precisely, I am excited at the role that Madge Hunter is playing in this room.

I imagine a quick dialogue in the car, as Earlene and Madge are driving home:

EARLENE: My brother Asa's in awful shape. Poor thing, he's shy.
MADGE: Doesn't he have a girl friend?

65

EARLENE: Oh, he did—a carhop, of all things, clear over on the other side of town, but she got married. He's very lonely, poor thing.

MADGE: Oh, that's too bad. Is he good-looking?

EARLENE: Well, *most* people certainly think so. Even though he's very shy, he's fantastically strong. I mean, very *physical*. Not to mention an astronomical I.Q. But you know how some men are with their intelligence. It just imprisons them. Or gets in their way, so they don't see what's going on under their very noses. Honestly!

MADGE: I know exactly what you mean.

EARLENE: I mean, he's working in a *produce* warehouse, with all these really *crummy* men. You should see them. Loading trucks, and things.

MADGE: Oh, I can imagine.

EARLENE: And he's so shy that he doesn't have any social life at all. It's very hard on him. I only wish he had a nice girl, someone to be nice to him.

MADGE: You mean, give him a good screwing when he needs it?

EARLENE (laughing): Precisely! That's *exactly* what I mean. Then maybe he wouldn't be so sarcastic with people. I mean, he would be more relaxed and happier.

MADGE: Well, I guess we women know how to take care of that! Is he home now?

EARLENE: Oh, I'm sure he is.

MADGE: Would you like me to come home with you? I'm not doing anything tonight. We can stop off and get my things. I've been wanting to meet this wonderful brother of yours for some time now.

EARLENE: Oh, Madge! *Would* you? Oh, that's just wonderful!"

66

My reverie is interrupted by a burst of laughter from Ear-lene. Madge has just uttered some jest that was lost in the radio jamming of my internal voices.

"Isn't it?" Earlene says, appealing to me to share in the fun.

"It certainly is," I agree, laughing like a jackass. Add to all my other sins the sin of dishonesty. Going along with the crowd. Moral spinelessness.

But the fact is, I will do anything at this moment: sign any document attesting to male chauvinism or sex as a neurotic fixation, personally legalize abortion, write slogans for FORCE. . . . Just name it, for I must have this candid woman's candid body. I have now focused upon her, for the first time (after the confusion of introductions—and a new face is always faintly traumatic to me), and I discover that she is without a bra. Her soft, warm breast is contoured for me as she gazes still upon the painting of St. Jerome (surely the jest had to do with him), and discusses it intelligently. The breast is just right—not too large, not too small. It is the size of a half a grapefruit, a well-veined muskmelon, or—for the cloacal—a toilet plunger. It is soft, and it rides comfortably low against her chest box. It is, I am certain, warmer near the armpit than it is at its convex extremity. The nipple, I suspect, is small and pert; although it might spread like an egg, for all I care, upon that warm and delicious sphere, and I will not complain. It may flower in any way it pleases, but flower it must.

Oh, gods! I am a monster in my lust! My sexual desire is itself the cause of its unfulfillment, for rutting in such a sweet field as this woman before me is too overwhelming, too important for me to take lightly, too glorious for me to be glib, or skillful, or even competent (beyond the physiological act, which I will stand against the potency of goats, boars, sweat bees, pigeons and fecund flies, m'lords).

Women blind me with their glories, so that I cannot cope with them. What Earlene says, with questionable validity, of my intelligence is surely true of my libido: the force of the thing itself prevents its fulfillment. Man is constructed in irony, and throughout his life, one half mocks the other.

I have gulped my beer—my third within an hour—and I am half-drunk.

Madge is sitting on a footstool, lecturing to us, saying merely intelligent things in a reasonable way, and Earlene is giving us all another beer. Roy is sitting, elbows on knees, a can of beer clasped equally in both hands before him—listening thoughtfully in his underwear.

Earlene's eyes are shining. The people (with the exception of Debra) who are most important to her are in her living room, drinking cold beer from her refrigerator, and talking warmly and interestedly to one another. Her brother, however, is tilted a little to the side, and cannot hear very well.

Asa Bean is half-loaded, anguished, suffering and contrite. He cannot follow what Madge is talking about. When there is a pause, he swallows a belch, and says, "Did you know that the Grand Doge of Venice was wedded to the sea?"

Earlene is the first to recover. "Whaaat?" she says.

Madge laughs. "Never mind," she says, "I recognize your brother's tactics. They're the oldest in the world, and *particularly* threatening to women. They're the well-known tactics of confusion."

"Right," Roy says, taking a drink.

That is a surprise. Roy has betrayed me? A defector? Or can he, too, conceivably have hot pants for old Madge?

"I have no tactics," I say. "I am artless, confused and afraid." Also, I am a little drunk, but I admit nothing about this.

"Hah!" Earlene says in derision.

68

"You have all the tactics of masculinity," Madge Hunter says with her eyes narrowed on me. I am in her sights, it is clear; and her manner is that of a super marksman.

Earlene says, gratuitously, "Listen to her, Asa."

"Like all women," Madge Hunter says, "I've had to become an expert diagnostician in this regard. And believe me, I've never seen an arsenal like yours."

"A what?" I ask.

Madge laughs, and then Earlene also laughs. A full beat later, Roy—the son-of-a bitch—joins them.

"Arsenal," Madge says. "See, Earlene? Even that is an example. Most women are confused by such diversionary tactics as that, but the time simply has come when we don't allow ourselves to be. Life is more than dialectics."

"Let me get that down on paper," I say, looking all around. But my sarcasm drifts off like smoke in a wind.

"Irony's at the heart of it," Madge says. "An inability to accept or reject anything fully. Women *have* to accept or reject, and that's the source of our maturity."

"She means 'maternity,'" I say to Roy, but old Roy isn't about to share a joke with me.

"Asa," Earlene says, "she's got your number."

"What do you mean?" I ask.

"You're always using the word 'irony.'"

"It's ironic you should think so," I say, "when I am innocent, artless, confused. . . ."

Earlene shrieks: "Stop him, Madge! He's doing it again!"

"I know, I know," Madge says.

"If you learn to look through two eyes," I say, "you'll learn to see things ironically. Binocular vision is what got us to where we are—mankind, I mean."

"Where *are* we?" Roy asks, trying a little irony himself.

"It's what civilizes us, goddamit! And all of you make me

sick, sitting around talking about my irony, for Christ's sake! You all sound like a bunch of goddam college sophomores. Now *there's* a group of more-or-less human creatures who don't know what irony is!"

"We're not talking about knowing what it is," Madge says. "We're talking about being *fixated* in it."

"That's right," Roy says.

"Oh shut up," I say.

"Nothing ironic about *that* statement," Roy says.

"Anything that gets through to you, you bonehead, can't be ironic."

"Now let's not get nasty," Earlene says.

"What I want to know," I say, articulating my words very slowly, "is why am I suddenly standing trial? Can anyone answer that?"

Something flashes in Madge's eyes. Some silent detonation and a brief flowering of light, from a depth charge going off deep in her ovaries and deep in her anfractuous brain, or deep in her carnivorous heart.

"For instance," she says, "why shouldn't I go over and sit beside Asa if I want to?"

Everybody looks at me as if a little surprised to see me sitting alone on the sofa.

Madge stands up, takes three heavy-heeled steps in my direction, and pivots upon one foot. "I ask you, why *shouldn't* I?"

Roy and Earlene watch. Madge's calf muscle swells gracefully in her outstretched leg. Asa the Pagan thinks of biting that golden calf. Certainly he already worships it. She looks like someone who has just taken the first, tentative step in a dance, and is waiting for the music to continue. And I suspect, or hope, that this is precisely what is happening.

She turns around, and still bearing that high-chinned smile, descends upon me and sits beside me on the sofa. I feel her hip pleasantly pinch against mine.

"Why shouldn't I *declare* my attraction for him, if I *feel* attraction?" she asks again. (I pray it is a rhetorical question.)

"Why not? Why not?"

"No reason," someone says. "No reason at all." It is myself who spoke.

Madge tilts her head toward me, and laughs silently. Now I can smell her perspiration. It is sweet, but definitely animal. I am shocked that she isn't wearing perfume; but I am interested. At this stage, I would forgive Madge anything. Not only that, it is *fresh* perspiration, and faintly aphrodisiac: Old Madge is steaming.

Earlene laughs with excitement. Her eyes, too, are shining. "Honestly," she says, sounding deliciously shocked, "do you two want Roy and me to leave you alone?"

"Yes," I say.

Again a maddening Madge laugh. She picks up my hand as if it were an empty glove, and twists it this way and that.

"Why don't you tell me some of your opinions about our organization?" she says. "You know, there are several intelligent and rather important *men* who are helping us out. Men who aren't *threatened* by women . . . that's what is required, of course. *You're* not threatened by women, are you?"

"No," I say. And then I wind up something in my mind, and say "As a matter of fact, Madge," (that's the first time I have spoken her name) "I consider myself distinctly . . . ah, uxorilocatropic. At least I have uxorilocatropic tendencies."

"Son of a bitch!" Roy exclaims.

Madge laughs again, which, if I were her manager, I would advise against. At least, I would recommend controlling the laugh. People don't like to think there are that many things that are funny. A laugh like that could put you out of medical school, even if you were a man.

"Now what does *that* mean?" Madge says, flicking an understanding (I swear, almost maternal) look at Earlene.

"Well," I say, "it has to do with kinship theory. 'Uxorilocal' is a word anthropologists use—"

"No anthropologist *I* know of," Madge interrupts.

"—anthropologists use to designate a kinship pattern in which the groom is expected—"

Madge pats my hand, and says, in the most tolerant of tones, "Asa, Asa, *Asa!*" until I stop.

"What is it?" I ask.

She shakes her head back and forth wonderingly. "You know, you play strange little games with people, don't you? Now let's be honest. You have a fantastic vocabulary, agreed; and you have a fantastic I.Q., agreed; and you have male, animal magnetism, agreed . . . but do you have to parade your *whole* arsenal *all* the time? Are you subconsciously trying to *scare people away, you're so threatened by them?*"

"Give it to him, Madge."

I am astonished. It is Roy who is cheering her on.

She pats my hand again and smiles. Her furry eyebrows look soft, and I would like to kiss them, four times each.

"Especially *women?*" Madge asks me.

"What's the subject?" I say.

"Oh, Asa," Earlene cries, "you're drunk!"

There was great disappointment in her voice.

Roy says, "Way to go, Ace!"

Suddenly, we are all quiet, and we sit there and breathe at one another (except Madge and I are breathing in parallax), and I am about to say, "All right, Madge, if you believe in sexual emancipation, come on up to my room and we'll settle

72

down to a night of *quid pro quo* screwing, or peer-group, sex."

The words, so help me, are about to dance out of my mouth, when Madge says, "Oh, God, it's after eleven o'clock. I've got to go."

I stand up, paralyzed, while phatic communion pops all around me; and the first thing I know is, the front door slams, Earlene is driving Madge home, Roy is pounding up the steps in his stocking feet, and I am standing alone, at attention, before the sofa, where Madge (more bitchy than butchy) left me only a few minutes before.

Eventually, I climb the steps to my bed. Utterly, you may be sure, discouraged.

19

One of the things about me that surprises me now and then is how tough I really am, when you come right down to it. I suppose my colossal incompetence and compulsive intellectuality fool a lot of people, including myself, into thinking I am really a sensitive flower.

Well, in a way I suppose I am. Certainly I seem to fall on the thorns of life a little more often than the average well-meaning creature, and I bleed pretty easily, but when the dawn comes, there's dumb old Asa Bean, bright-eyed and bushy-tailed, ready to go out and test more thorns.

So I cursed myself asleep after Madge Hunter left, but when morning came (it was Sunday, and I slept till nine o'clock), I was downstairs eating breakfast. Everything was the same, except I got the feeling that Earlene was casting meaningful looks at me, now and then, but I couldn't for the life of me decode her messages. When she took Madge home last night, I am sure the two of them did some serious female gabbing, and I seriously doubt if it was about FORCE. And yet, it seems downright conceited of me to assume I was the topic under discussion.

I envisioned a few more dialogues, tending to eventuate in unlikely erotic scenes, and sipped my morning coffee. Roy was talking about an apartment-house sale that he thought he might be able to close sometime today. He works harder on Sunday than on any other day.

After breakfast, Roy leaves, and I lounge around the house (female), reading from several journals, a new novel that Earlene got from a book club, and several other things; also stopping periodically to go take a leak or stand in back and try to remember exactly where the mums (female) were growing last fall.

When I return to my reading after such a journey, Earlene comes up and plants herself right in front of me, without speaking, until I look up and see her staring at me.

"What is it?" I ask.

"Asa, how did you like Madge?"

"A very interesting woman," I say.

"Do you really think so?"

"Sure. I do."

"I mean, she didn't come on too strong for you or anything, did she?"

"No. I thought she was just fine. Interesting person."

Earlene rolls her eyes, and says, "God, is she dedicated! And *intelligent!* A *genius,* Asa! Do you know what she observed about my name? It's a man's name, and represents what we're talking about all along, you know? That women are sort of forced into being second-class men. Like 'Earl' is a man's name, and why should it have to be *my* name, too? I mean, you just put 'e–n–e' on the end of it, and—zap—it's a girl's name. But it isn't really, you know. It's no more than a hand-me-down. That's all it is."

"Sure," I say. "There's a certain unquestionable validity to what you say. At least, nominally. Of course, there's something tricky in that."

"What?" Earlene says, wary.

"Well, it has to be pointed out that if all this business about 'Earlene' as a woman's name is true—its being imitation male, or whatever—than as a man's name it's true, also: I mean, the same argument would have men being considered second-hand Earls in terms of the name."

"Oh, Asa, that's not the same thing."

I don't feel like arguing the point, so I admit that there is the faint odor of sophistry in what I've said, mercifully ignoring the similar taint in Madge Hunter's analysis.

"I'm glad you didn't think Madge came on too strong," Earlene says. "She was kind of afraid she might have."

"You mean, the two of you talked about me after you left?" I ask.

Earlene's eyes sparkle. "Oh, sure. We had to talk about *something,* you know."

She pauses and looks secretively at the ceiling, a smug little smile puckering her cheeks.

"I'll tell you what, Asa: you better watch out."

"Why?"

"I think Madge has her eye on you."

I sit there and meditate, with my mouth turning dry, while Earlene returns to the kitchen. If the two of them only knew! But then, maybe they do.

20

Asa the Aphorist once said, "Intelligence is not manifest in the total absence of confusion, but in the level of complexity at which confusion is the ineluctable result."

Now that is a very dangerous idea, for it can serve as an excuse for not achieving clarity. An excuse always weakens, especially when it makes *some* claim to validity; and the above statement *is* true, in a way, and once understood, will always try to seduce our minds away from their heroic pilgrimages to the cities of clarity, where truth and beauty (yes, this is beautifully, clearly true) reside.

Confusion riots in my mind. The Anarchist, Shawnee and Assassin have gamboled through the newsreels of my dreams, leaving me empty and bewildered when the alarm rings at four A.M. I arise, shuffle on my clothes, wash my face and hands (beard dribbling water all over my collar, so that I will be wearing a ring of ice when I arrive at Mitch's Café, where I usually bolt down my breakfast, alone, growling in my beard).

I go to the corner of Marlborough and Lexington Boulevard, where an Owl bus stops once an hour. I climb aboard, and see the same old faces that never show recognition at this desolate, dark hour in the morning (and who could blame them?). I open a volume of the Pound translation of the Confucian *Analects,* and prepare to read for the next eighteen minutes, until the bus (female) deposits me at Mitch's restaurant, where I will ensconce myself in a warm booth (female) and engorge a monstrous breakfast.

It is about a half mile from the bus stop to Mitch's, and I know that by the time I arrive there, I will have tears in my eyes from the cold.

So be it.

For some reason, I am three minutes late, and for another reason, when I have finished breakfast, Durango, Tubbs and Wilbur are already at work. Four trailers are backed up against the dock, and two of them are idling, vomiting diesel exhausts into the black winter air, while their drivers sleep in the cabs, waiting for their trailers to be loaded.

One of them, named Faraday, gets out of the cab and comes toward me sleepily, asking what time it is. I tell him it's just five after, and he nods, shivers, and then darts inside the warehouse.

Durango roars by me on a bug, sees me, holds six fingers up and shouts, "Sylvia, last night."

Then he coasts around a corner, and I am left standing, tying my denim apron to my waist.

"What's up?" I say to Wilbur. Wilbur points at the order board, which is fluttering with load sheets in the draft from an overhead register. "Help yourself," he says. "Charley has to be loaded by six. You better get his first."

I nod, and then immerse myself in the load: sixteen crates of bananas; twenty-two 100-pound bags of potatoes; thirty-three cartons of hothouse tomatoes; sixteen sacks of cabbages; etc.; etc.

Now we go to the banana room to hang bananas. The room is kept at a steady sixty-six degrees for controlled ripening, and it is nothing but a large, cement vault with wired lights protruding like abstractionist nipples from the ceiling. We hang the bunches of green bananas (the bunches ranging from sixty to 150 pounds) alternately from ceiling hooks and noosed ropes. A two-step stool is shoved around on the floor so we can climb and reach the ceiling hooks.

The room is warm and fragrant with the rich odor of bananas. Soon we are sweating out our breakfast juices, and grunting and voiding casual obscenities with our meaty efforts, bumping the great pendulous fruits and bruising them with the happy, brainless contempt that is born of plenitude.

Once a month, one of us will plunge our hands into a bunch, groping for the heavy stalk, and feel a soft breath over the hand, and maybe even see the banana spider that traced its woolly legs over our skin. But most of the spiders have been killed by spraying and dipping a week before, or by the sudden cold; and at any rate, they do not bite.

When we finish loading the banana room, we go our separate ways, on separate chores. I climb upon a bug and start for the front office, where I am to enquire about a boxcar load of sugar that grocery needs help with.

When I turn a corner around the Great Northern Tissue section, I almost run into Linda Thorpe, the redheaded secretary whom Wilbur is always going up to flirt with.

She jumps aside and laughs a scared little, thrilled little, I-want-to-get-screwed-right-away, girl laugh.

"Oh, I thought you were going to run over me," she cries, when I idle the bug. The engine is missing a little, so all that she says is accompanied by the snort and pop of the idling bug.

"I was looking for you, as a matter of fact," she says. "Here. You got some mail."

She holds out a letter, stamped and addressed to "Asa Bean, c/o The A & P Warehouse, Granger Road, City."

"It looks like a girl's handwriting," Linda Thorpe says, smiling a naughty smile at me.

"Yes, it does," I answer, with what is tantamount to extraordinary intelligence in Asa Bean's recent uptight conversation.

"Well," Linda says, "I'll leave you alone, now that I've delivered your letter."

She arcs a little smile at me, and suddenly I take a better look at her. Not only is she a redhead, but she has a sweet, round face that appears to have just been pinched all over. Her mouth looks like it is sucking ginger ale through a straw, and her eyes are a pale, bold blue.

"Ta, ta," she says, and pivots on her heel.

For an instant, I visualize speeding up to her on the bug and swinging her up into the saddle, the way cowboys used to do in movies, and whipping her up a dark aisle down the line, where I would throw her upon my personal (*geistiges eigentum*) 140-pound bean sacks (yes, *Bean* sacks), and plumb her vibrant depths with a furious fandango of erotic ploys.

But the fantasy evaporates (the only defect in fantasies), and I am abandoned to the letter in my hand.

While the bug engine idles and burps and bubbles beneath my feet, I open the letter and read:

Dear Asa:

I do hope you are not angry with me for "standing you up" the other day. As I explained in my note, my father had a nasty fall, and for a while they were afraid he had broken his leg, but it turned out that he was hardly hurt at all. Still, you never know, and that is why they called me. But as it turned out, he hardly limps at all, and the doctors said there was nothing wrong but a bruise.

Anyway, I just wanted you to know that it was nothing that could be helped, and it *certainly wasn't anything personal.* I do hope you understand.

Sincerely,
Veronica Talbot

Well. That makes things seem a lot more interesting. I probe the diction for signs of a benign and subtle irony. Where would the emphasis fall? I listen to Veronica in my imagination, with the hope of hearing the word "wanted" emphasized (grunted, hissed in the rictus of climactic ecstasy): the "sincerely" might conceal, beneath the banal ceremonial function, a mocking allusion to Veronica's being *able and willing and indeed anxious to give all!*

"Hey, Soy Bean!"

It is, of course, Durango. And simultaneous with the sound of his voice is the roar of his well-oiled bug as he coasts it up alongside mine (Sheriff A. Bean and the Durango Kid sitting side by side in their saddles, frowning out upon the sun-drenched slopes before them, while in the distance a soft plume of dust rests upon the clear desert air).

"Hey, Man, Wilbur wants to know you found out about that sugar load yet."

"I'm on my way now."

Veronica will have to wait.

I am about to leave for the front office, when Durango reaches over and grabs my arm. "Hey, Soy Bean," he says, lowering his voice a little, "six times last night. With Sylvia. Six times."

"In the Mustang?" I ask.

"Oh hell no. At her house. She lives with this other broad, who wasn' home. She's sackin up with some guy got a house down in Florida."

"Sounds great," I say, meaning both words.

"Great is what it was," Durango says, his eyes distant with the memory of nooky. Then he says, "Any time you wan' use the Mustang, Man, it's okay'th me."

"Sure. Thanks." For an instant, I think of asking if I can borrow Sylvia, too, but before I can speak, Durango peels off, giving a thumbs-up sign before he goes down the very bean-sack row where Linda Thorpe has just been ravished eighteen times by Randy Old Fant-assed Asa Bean.

Asa Bean now revs up his engines, and speeds toward the front office for instructions. Where he finds out that, yes, the grocery section needs help in unloading the boxcar of sugar, so that Tubbs, Wilbur, Durango and Asa Bean will soon be working in a slightly different section of the warehouse microcosm.

All that afternoon I think about Veronica's letter. I think of Veronica, and realize that she hardly ever smiles, whereas Madge Hunter (from my brief exposure to her) seems to send out beams as compulsively and as consistently as an oscillating buoy upon the dark oceans of this confusing world. At least she sent out beams to me, Asa Bean.

Is it conceivable that I need them both? That they are complements to each other, sisters, meant to be sacrificed upon the altars of Asa M. Bean's demonic lust?

21

Just before quitting time, in a manic surge, I phone Veronica and ask if I can pick her up when she gets off work, and take her to dinner. I am a little low on money, but maybe Roy will lend me ten dollars. Otherwise, I'll use a credit card.

It is shortly after the noon hour when I call . . . barely afternoon. And when the phone is ringing, I realize that this is inconsiderate of me, that my phone call will probably cause her to lose a dollar in tips.

Then that strikes me as ridiculous (all this speeded up in

81

the film of my mind, while the phone is buzzing). A waitress' voice I don't recognize answers, and I ask for Veronica.

A short wait, and then Veronica herself answers, and sounds relaxed and perfectly happy to be interrupted, and accepting of my invitation.

I am hollowed out, rendered weightless by this *fait accompli*. I am not accustomed to decisiveness in my actions.

I am dizzy, distrait, slightly removed from it all. When Durango lets me off at the bus stop, I can't remember a word he has said, although I know he has been talking constantly since we left the warehouse.

I go home from work—very tired from fantasies and work —and take a hissing (mine) hot bath. I dry myself, comb my beard, and then lie down in my bed to steam and groan and breathe and hopefully to nap.

Strangely, I begin to think of Madge Huntress. Goddess excellently bright (for she *is* intelligent, beyond question). And then I think of an article I once started to write on Sophocles' *Trachiniae*. It had to do with Deianira's robe, and some latent symbolism in the robe, and the relationship between Deianira and Hercules (archetypal female/male), and now, retroactively, all this had something to do with FORCE.

FORCE was in my thinking because Earlene, when I first stepped in the house, had come up to me and said, "We have decided on our demonstration! But it will have to remain a secret, of course."

She was so excited, she kept licking her lips and running her hand through her hair.

Since Earlene is a member of the Board of Directors of the local chapter of FORCE, I asked if that was what the word "we" referred to, and she said yes.

"How many on this broad board?" I asked.

"Five."

82

I nodded and said, "It'll be a miracle if five women can keep a secret for over two hours and fifteen minutes."

That made her mad, and she gave me a quick scorching lecture for thinking in stereotypes, and being condescending, and all that.

"You're *so* sure of yourself," she said, scornfully.

I could have cried when she said that, but I managed to keep a straight face and look arrogant.

Then Earlene said something that later struck me as a little strange and out of context: "You men are going to have to stop considering women as *mere sex objects!*"

Was that my chief failing in life? Was that a clue to this mysterious demonstration the girls were planning? (The Anarchist, the Shawnee and the Assassin pause and look up, interested and wary; a vixen lowers her delicate muzzle to the ground and touches the spore of Glooscap, the Mad Hare.)

"Look," I said, "it's all right with me if you have a soul, Sheherazade. I'd like one myself, but ladies first."

That was three hours ago, exceeding my prediction of how long the five FORCE board broads could keep the secret of their eye-opening demonstration, that was—one assumed—imminent.

I still don't know what they have in mind, but I am not even thinking of FORCE now. I am thinking of Veronica Talbot. My image is throwing her image into all sorts of erotic positions, and rogering her again and again and again.

When I descend the stairs, I hear Roy speaking about the apartment-house sale, which has hung fire, and I drink a quick cup of coffee (left over from lunch) before throwing on my clothes and charging out into the cold.

I take a bus to Durango's house, pick up the Mustang, and then head for The Fifth Wheel, where Veronica is probably right at this instant combing her rich brown spun-molasses hair and staring incuriously out upon that Düreresque countenance in the mirror . . . the countenance that so fires the seething furnace of Asa Bean's ardour. Solid-footed, heavy-hammed, warm with the abundance of her own pale meats . . . skin faintly glowing from the heat of carrying cold bottles of beer to numberless, nameless, surly studs, who do not so much as deserve to have her cool eyes rest upon them.

I park Durango's Mustang once again, and head for the Mother Goose gable. I walk in, and Craig Todhunter waves to me. The place is filled with drinkers and diners, male and female. The jukebox is uncoiling a window-cracking counterpoint into the big room, reverberating with a ponderous bass.

Veronica is standing with her coat on, back by the corner of the bar. She is simply looking at me, with her hands clasped in front of her, wearing a magic robe of silence in all this noise. On one of her fingers, there is a Band-Aid . . . supposed to be skin color, but lighter by one shade than Veronica's soft, pale integument.

Her expression is impassive, tolerant and (I think) wise. Under her coat lie those two great land masses, the Peloponnesus and Crete, and in between the sacred island of Cythera.

Motionless, Veronica awaits my coming, indifferent to the fantastic geographies I make of her; and I approach.

22

There is a fabled land, out of space and out of time, which sends forth upon its constant surging floods great galleons, argosies, brigantines and caravels, wallowing waist-deep in the dark waters, burdened joyously with cargoes of ambrosial corn, spice, sweet oils, minerals and nectareous wines.

This is the land of fancy, and it is difficult for me to imagine a busier port than Asa M. Bean's imagination in the receiving of such shipments. And how likely but sad it is that after such flourishing and busy-ness, there should be so many desolate moments in the warehouses and granaries in the hinterland, when it is found that the ambrosial grain is really cankerous, the sweet oils rancid, and the nectareous wine vitiated with brackish water.

It is not that Veronica is a disappointment to me; the problem is more precisely the disappointment of the two of us together. We do not harmonize. We really make no particular noise at all. Occasionally I pause in my eating and look at her, but hear neither the sound of breath nor the sound of chewing.

Can so much gloried flesh be impalpable?

I have brought her to this restaurant that is strikingly like The Fifth Wheel. She twirls her glass of rosé in the hand with the Band-Aid on the finger. She looks vaguely content, vaguely interested, vaguely vague . . . where Madge Hunter is, in so many important ways, fair, Veronica Talbot is vague.

We talk. Asa Bean's profundities sound like platitudes; his platitudes resonate like oracles. Our pan-fried steaks arrive, and we discuss various topics. All the topics are red herrings, feints, unselective signaling to conceal Asa Bean's morbid, vital preoccupation with his vision of Cythera.

Veronica stirs on her seat in the booth, some nerve in her body receiving the delicious warning signal that she is under attack. The Peloponnesus and Crete are tantalized by subterrene tremors, and the Holy Island feels a warm darkness blink over the solar apogee of noon.

The gift of metaphor brings me alive. To know what

something is *like* is to know its essence. All things exist in association; therefore to know their quiddities, we must know their possible, as well as their actual, relations.

The Dürer mask jumps into life. I am once more aware of the game we are playing, the game we are condemned to play, by a holy, infinitely subtle, grand but frolicsome Deity.

The woman herself appears jejune, inane. A desert of mirrored absences, wherein winds of loss blow with the breath of midnight, and carry flatulent gases from forgotten temples.

But I am not deceived. If the two of us can survive these desperate first moments of boredom, during which our eyeless citadels stare blankly upon each other, we will know passion together and hear the song of the morning stars.

There are fits and cadenzas of talk during our meal, however, and somewhere behind or beneath Veronica's wholesome peasant beauty, there is a mystery residing. She is unmarried (and at least twenty-five), and she keeps house for her father, who is a traveling salesman—a seller of class rings and pins to high schools, and watches, pens, and sundries to small businesses and organizations.

I take her to a movie, where we are immersed in passionate music and the charade of steatomammarous women in various stages of rut. They are all strangely epicene behind their silicone tits, however, for who can really forget the cameramen, crews, extras, and the whole legion of deceptors whose fabrications produced these public fantasies? (I know the enemy; I can smell his spoor.)

The excitement comes from Veronica, and the thought that *she* might be excited. It is the warm, real presence beside me, and not the cool public shadows before us, that contains the seedbed and the truth. Even that cunning old fairy Plato knew the difference.

After the movie, I guide Veronica into Durango's Mustang, where I kiss her on the mouth. She opens her lips for me, and of course that is symbolic (or of course it is symbolic to Asa Bean). I fondle, caress, rub her breasts with my hand, and she puts one of her hands behind my head. It is too cold for me to put my hand inside her dress.

"Is your father home?" I ask her.

She shakes her head. "He shouldn't be. He's out of town, and I don't think he'll be back tonight. But I don't think we should go in. Not tonight."

I am driving carefully through the streets, which have been cleared. The dirty clumps of snow lining the gutters look like the metal sculpture of a score of anonymous madmen.

Veronica lives in an apartment building about two miles away. She says she walks to work, sometimes, when the weather is good.

"Don't lose weight," I whisper under my breath. I don't want to be deprived of a pound, even an ounce, of her callipygian splendor.

23

The apartment building is handsome, made of smooth brick, painted white and decorated with filigreed black shutters on the windows. When we enter, however, the opulence evaporates. The carpet is tattered, and on one of the walls there is an angry display of imbecilic crayon art—demented scrawls and coils and zig-zags.

We rise upon the stairway together, and Veronica leans over, her ear to the door (the femininity of her stance and expression a sudden delicious pain in my heart) as she plucks with her key at the keyhole. She fumbles, frowns, looks dismayed (all in an instant), and I take the key from her cold hand and jam it into the keyhole (female), and turn it with a visceral grinding of the latch and guard bolt, and the door sighs and lets go.

Veronica shoots a quick sad smile at me, and for the first time we are natural with each other. This waitress is not at ease when she sits in a booth and has another woman wait on her. How could I have been so obtuse as not to know this profound truth?

We step inside a small apartment, the right wall rubbing against my shoulder, saying, "Be gentle with this woman, be wise; but above all be true and be thorough."

Fantasies dissipate when she flicks on the light-switch, but only to be replaced by another system of fantasies: the small room, one side dominated by an enormous L-shaped sofa, pathetically modernistic and worn; the inevitable planter separating this area from the kitchen; a single inert mobile of copper fins hanging from the ceiling; an enormous old-fashioned television set, with the china figurine of a cat, prone and curled up like a hairy little moon, on top; the odor of inutility and dust and loneliness.

"Well," Veronica says, looking out upon the scene with a discovery that must be a muted version of my own, "this is where I live."

I take her coat off, and she asks if I would like a cup of coffee.

"No," I say, but sounding strangely unlike myself (like Rock Hudson, perhaps, reciting a bad line), "but I would like this!"

I turn her toward me and kiss her long and hard on the mouth. Again, her lips ease open, but then she pulls back and groans, "No. Not now. Not tonight. I'm sorry."

But I am hugging her and kissing her again, and finally my hand swims inside her clothes at the neckline, and I am cupping her naked left breast in my hand. Her dress is practically choking her at the neck, and her eyes are closed. Maybe she is about to faint from loss of blood supply to the head.

"No, no, no," she recites.

Suddenly, her voice comes through to me and I stop, looking at her.

"Oh, you do turn me on," she says. "I mean, you really do, but we can't tonight."

For an instant, I am perplexed. I take a stupid breath and exhale, my hands slipping down upon each of her glorious hips.

Taking a deep breath, she casts her eyes imploringly to the ceiling, and turns away from me. "Oh why do I have to get so hot when it's my *period!*" she cries.

The revelation seems to dismay us both, equally. My hands drop to my sides, and I stand there looking at her face. But she doesn't look back.

"Today isn't the end of the world, though," she says. "I mean, there are other days. And I did enjoy myself tonight. I mean, it isn't like I don't *like* you!"

She seems to hate herself, for reasons over which she can't possibly have any control.

"You must think I'm awful," she says, caressing my right hand with both of hers. I raise the hand to my mouth and kiss it, and with her other she pats the back of my head.

It is a screwy, screwless, screwloose scene, I think.

Then she takes a deep breath and says, "Let me make you a cup of coffee, at least. That's the least I can do for you."

She seems almost ready to cry, and of course I agree to the coffee.

She walks out into the kitchen, and I stand there feeling so sorry for her I can almost taste the pain. And yet, there is something good about it, too: Asa Bean is capable of pity and tenderness toward this woman, and the son of a bitch happens to be perceptive enough to know this, and to know all the possible stances toward the fact, so that he is pleased and a little annoyed with his ambivalent pleasure.

When Veronica brings the coffee into the front room, I almost ask her to marry me; but fortunately I keep my mouth shut.

Then she sits down beside me, pats my hand, and we both take a sip of coffee together.

At that precise instant, there is a scrabbling sound at the door, as if a giant crab is attacking the wood with claws the size of Coke bottles.

Veronica's eyes unfocus and her face goes pale. "Daddy," she whispers.

Then there is the sound of a key in the lock, and once more the door gives in and swings open.

A stocky man in his early sixties stumbles in, still hanging onto the front knob with one hand and holding a golf club in the other. His face is red and blotched, and there is a ski cap on his head—very much like mine, as a matter of fact. The father and daughter do not speak to each other, but for a brief moment they measure the distance between them, and I am aware that they know each other's faults and habits well.

"I'm Jim Talbot," he says, after he swings the door shut. "I'm her father." He waves the golf club in the direction of Veronica, who is still sitting on the sofa, gripping her hands together. She cracks her knuckles and says, "Some father!"

"She's my daughter," Jim Talbot says redundantly. And then, as if to clarify everything and clear up any possible confusion or dissident opinion, he says, "I'm her father."

"What's that?" Veronica says, pointing to the golf club.

90

"That is a golf club," he says. He gives it a little swing, and then lifts the head in front of his face and looks at it cross-eyed. "A putter," he says.

"Where did you get it?" Veronica asks.

"I won it on a bet," he answers, giving it another neat little swing.

"I've never known you to play golf."

"It's been years," Jim Talbot says. "Many, many years." He sways largely to the side, and then grabs his thigh, groaning with pain. "Any golf balls around this place?"

"Of course not," Veronica says. "You're home, now. Remember? You know there aren't any golf balls around here."

"You can never tell," Jim Talbot says. "You can never tell."

"Dumb," Veronica says.

"No harm in asking, is there?" He looks at her with raised eyebrows.

"You're crazy," she says.

He takes another swing, with the head of the club turned halfway around, and then hands the club to me. "Let's see your form," he says.

"What?" I ask him.

"Your form. You know: that's what they call your style in the swing. Your golf form. Let's see how you wield the old putter."

I pick up the club and look at the head. "This is a number-three iron," I say.

"Putter," Jim Talbot says. "Putter."

"But it's too long for a putter," I tell him. "Not only that, it has number three marked on it."

"Number-three putter for a tall man," he says. "Probably, if the truth were known, a custom-made putter." He appears unfazed by my challenge. In fact, he jams his hand in his right pant pocket and pulls out two white ballpoint pens, and hands them to me. "Here," he says. "Be my guest."

I thank him and read "Altmeier Printing Company" printed on the pens. "What is it?" I ask fatuously.

"I'm in advertising," Jim Talbot says.

"Big business man," Veronica says. "Honestly!"

"Well," her father says, as if answering an inaudible question, "my leg seems to be healing all right. They thought it was broken when I fell. Yes, thought it was broken."

"He knows, he *knows!*" Veronica says, repeating the paternal compulsion to repeat.

"It was just a bruise, though." He squints his eyes and gazes drunkenly at a far-distant wall somewhere.

"You never give up, do you?" Veronica asks him.

But her old man doesn't hear; his mind overshoots her question and lands on less tangible things. Then he says, "We're all survivors. Ever think of that? We're all survivors. Every one of us. Survivors of something, at least. Think about it."

"*You're* the world champion survivor, though," Veronica says. "Nobody survives the way you do."

"Played golf long?" he asks me.

"I don't play golf at all," I tell him; but he obviously doesn't hear me, and says, "I think maybe I'll go back to it myself. It's been many, many, many years. Many, many years. Yes, I'm getting interested in the game once more. How about you and me playing a round as soon as the weather clears up a little?"

He's looking at me with such an intent expression that I don't know what to say. But Veronica does: she says, "For God's sake, it's zero weather out there, and here you are talking about playing *golf!*"

"Every winter turns to spring, hon."

92

I glance at him to see if he knows he's quoting Tennyson, but his face is a marvel of surface. The face knows nothing. And possibly the brain, too.

"Men!" Veronica says, including me in the vortex of her father's eccentricity. (Asa Bean, the Paradoxist.)

"Who are *you*," he says, gesturing grandly, and his voice rising, "to legislate *my* interests?"

"You'd never get past the nineteenth hole," she says contemptuously.

"Very witty, very witty. It so happens, the 'nineteenth hole' is one more than is necessary to play the game."

"Not for you, it wouldn't be," Veronica says.

"Very funny," he says. Then his eyes come back to me, and he says, "And what is that name again, may I ask?"

"Whose name?"

"*Your* name."

"Asa Bean," I say. We shake hands, and I say, "Asa M. Bean."

"Ah, Asa *M*. Bean." His tone suggests that now he can distinguish me from scores of other Asa Beans populating the area.

"That's right," I say, grinning idiotically.

He bids us good night, ambles back through the kitchenette to his bedroom, and suddenly I am aware—briefly reflecting upon the whole mad scene—that we are always reduced to the level of the least among us. Who can resist insanity?

But surely I am not as colossally silly as this drunken golfer *manqué!* Surely, surely!

Even if he does wear a hat strikingly like mine.

Veronica and I resume our places on the sofa, side by side, like two strangers waiting for different flights at O'Hare Field.

And before I can think of an intelligent phatic ploy, her father is calling out from the back room.

"Oh hell," she says. But dutifully she arises, and dutifully goes back to where the old bastard is now ensconced with pontifical authority.

I sit there and grind my teeth until Veronica returns. She doesn't look at me, but holds out five or six more of the ball-point pens, advertising the Altmeier Printing Company.

"Here," she says, "he wants you to have these."

"He already gave me some," I say.

"Yes, but he wants you to have some more."

I take the pens and shove them in my pocket. "Is that why he called you just now?"

"Yes," Veronica says. Then she giggles, looking me straight in the eyes. It is an astonishing transformation for the Dürer mask to undergo. I can hardly believe it.

But here I am, in Veronica's apartment, my pockets stuffed with Altmeier Printing Company ballpoints, my genitals swollen with unnatural and prolonged abstinence, my head whirling with verbal fantasies, arpeggios of recondite association, infinite resources of image and chord.

I am a seventy-eight piece band, blaring forward into the fortuities of each moment.

Bean, the Heuristicist.

We talk.

We kiss.

I leave.

Durango's Mustang is slow in starting. I take it to an all-night Texaco station, where I have it filled with regular.

Then I drive home.

Astonished most of all, perhaps, by the inextirpable thought of Veronica's sudden giggle as she handed me the Altmeier ballpoint pens.

24

The instincts of the average man are quite correct when he looks at the intellectual, that card-carrying alien in any society, and brands him as a footnote, an irrelevant clown, a sneeze in church or production line. The intellectual's existence is essentially comic, in the frame of reference of the average man, and of course it is this frame of reference that we must all more or less accept, or be institutionalized.

The antistrophe to this, however, is that the existence of the average man is always pathetic. Of course this realization is limited to intellectuals, for the most part, and occasionally to religious hysterics, saints, political (as well as cultural) aliens, an occasional drunk, and—to be candid, and simplify the list—almost anyone, now and then, when the chemistry of his life and conditions are right.

A good intellectual (by which I mean an honest one, who chooses the schizoid existence of world and ideas) will be an average man grown up, or at least grown out, to include this alien for whom words and ideas are as real as the car generator and the transistor radio.

Asa Bean, the Alien, lives his life, endures his *non sequiturs,* swallows his lies, and glories in his contingencies and serendipities, pretty much as others do. His intellectual part presides over his fate distinctly more often than is average, or even "normal," but his beautiful, dumb, faithful horse of a body is always following obediently behind, ready for the tired cerebral trailblazer to climb aboard and nod ahead on any journey demanded by the quotidian exigencies of this life.

Thus it is that he now stands near the time clock, waiting for the minute hand to jump forward three more times, so that he can insert his card, stamp it, and legally end another eight-hour workday.

For most of these eight hours, I have been replaying last night's scene with Veronica and her father. In every dark aisle of groceries, I have come upon Jim Talbot's *Doppelgänger* holding a bouquet of cheap ballpoints, or maybe taking a few practice swings with a number-three putter.

Once, I envisioned Veronica, Durango and myself, marching like Dulcinea, Sancho Panza and Don Quixote into the art museum. It was a fabulous scene, jumping into adventitious focus right by the second row of orange crates, where I had only two days before asked the skylights: "What is it that women really *want?*"

This warehouse is my art museum, the art museum my warehouse.

Our formulations are such—as Oscar Wilde discovered—that they almost inevitably give up interesting and surprising meanings when they are simply reversed.

"Work is the curse of the drinking class," for example.

Or, as I have so often thought: "The last animal to be tamed is man . . . by woman" is no more interesting, no more provocative than: "The last animal to be tamed is woman . . . by man."

The Greeks would have understood this, for it is the source of dialectic. Or the Gestalt psychologists, for figure insists upon becoming background, and background insists upon becoming figure.

Or Hegel.

Oh, but it has been a typical day. An intensely, surprisingly, uncommonly typical day.

Asa Bean, both man and horse, worked together; it was

96

merely the horse that had his way. To address him, however, is always to bring the man awake, precisely as a lamp reveals only one thing, no matter where its beams are directed: light.

Durango is standing behind me, smoking a cigarette. I hear a long exhalation, and the sound indicates that he is about to speak.

"Hey, Soy Bean, I got a question."

I turn around, and as I do so, the minute hand clicks forward one more minute.

"Yes?" I ask.

"Kin' of crazy question to ask," Durango says, looking slightly over my right shoulder. "But you seem to like crazy questions."

"Sure," I say. "I thrive on them; and as a matter of fact, I ask a lot of them myself."

Durango frowns. "That's what I mean, you know? You always askin these here crazy goddam questions, so I thought I ask you one."

"Which is?"

"Which is, exactly what *is* a goddam soy bean?"

"It's a vegetable. Like the name says, a bean. Grows on a little vine, like lima beans."

Durango's frown deepens. "Yeah, but what the fuck, man, we don' get no soy beans in here. Not that I ever heard of. We get other kinds of beans, but how's come no *soy* beans? What they do with the fuckin things? Beans are produce, right? I mean, nobody ever heard of soy bean soup or soy bean salad or soy bean pie or nothin like that."

"It's a special kind of bean," I say. "They've got a hundred commercial uses for them. They make forage out of them— you know, food for cows and pigs. They squeeze the juice out of them, for oils—like margarine; and they use the mash for different things—some kinds of plastics, for example. They

97

even make a broth out of it as a culture to grow streptomycin in—you know, one of the wonder drugs."

Durango nods, and then shakes his head sideways. "Man, don' you get a headache rememberin all them things?"

"No," I tell him. "I get a headache when I'm not getting enough to remember."

The minute hand clicks over to one-thirty, and Wilbur rings his card out, and then I ring mine, and then Durango rings his. Tubbs was twenty minutes late, so he is working overtime in grocery to make it up.

"You wanna drink a beer?" Durango says.

"No, I'm almost broke."

"Me, too," Durango says. "Come on, I'll give you a lift to the fuckin bus stop."

I get in the Mustang, and wait while Durango wipes his glove over the front windshield, unravelling a thin film of snow like soft old tatters and strips of white underwear.

Then he gets in the car and whistles all the way to the traffic light at the entrance, where he starts cussing, because the Mustang doesn't sound a bit good in the idle. It needs a valve job, anybody could tell.

When Durango lets me off at the bus stop, I lean out over the curb to peer around a parked car, wondering how long I will have to wait for the next bus to Marlborough Heights.

Suddenly, there is a familiar car right in front of me, and the driver is energetically signaling me to get in before the light changes.

Of course I recognize him: it is old Roy, identifiable even though he is fully dressed and not drinking a beer. He says, "I was hoping to pick you up, Ace."

Something troubled and/or authoritative in his tone makes me wary. "You don't have to take me home," I say.

"Listen," Roy says, "I *want* to take you home. As a matter

of fact, I was on my way to the warehouse to pick you up, because I wanted to have a chance to talk with you when Earlene isn't around. But I was held up by the goddam traffic."

The streets are still slippery here and there in spite of all the salt the city has been spreading, and our car skids a little as Roy pulls to a stop behind another car. He honks his horn at it, as if it shouldn't be stopped for the traffic light. It could be dangerous, stopping in front of my brother-in-law.

"A family," Roy says, "is like a finely tuned mechanism. When one part gets out of whack, all the other parts are affected."

"Did you learn that from Marx?" I ask. "Lenin? Trotsky? Che Guevara? Mao?"

"Listen," Roy says, "don't turn everything into a joke. I want to be serious for a minute."

"Shit," I say. "I mean, 'shoot.' Incidentally, did you know that the two words are cognate?"

"What?"

" 'Shit' and 'shoot.' "

"Listen," Roy says, "I don't give a shit for 'shit' and 'shoot.' So will you please be quiet?"

"I'll keep my mouth shut," I say.

Some wild conceit almost makes him bang into the back of another car. He honks his horn and says, "I wish to hell these boneheads knew how to drive!"

"Continue," I say, when he has finally extricated the car from a temporary thicket of traffic.

"As I was saying," he says, "when one person in a family is off, it throws everybody else off."

"You are speaking of me," I say.

"Yes, Ace, I am speaking of you."

"What's wrong now?"

"The same old thing, Ace. You know what's wrong as

99

well as I do. And believe me, it upsets Earlene. And, of course, if *she's* upset, so's Debra. It all comes back to you, Ace. You are suffering from one of the worst cases of that famous Japanese disease, 'Lack-o'-nooky,' I have ever had the misfortune to witness. And I'll tell you why."

I turn and gaze at Roy's profile: his lips are sucked in and he is nodding with profound recognition at the truth of what he is about to convey.

"Why?" I ask him.

"The reason is, Ace, you are too analytical. I can see it as plain as the nose on your face: you scare women away with your ways of speaking and acting. You make them uncomfortable. Hell, as a matter of fact, you make *anybody* uncomfortable. Not just women. And of course, nothing's as delicate as trying to make a broad, you know what I mean?"

I sit there groping for some memory or reference, but I am tired and filled with despair and disgusted and frustrated. Roy hits the brakes again, and the car eases sideways as we skid within one foot of another car ahead.

"You're tail-gating," I say.

"Never mind me," Roy says, "we're talking about you."

"Asa Bean," I say.

I can tell he gives me a long disgusted look as the light changes again.

"If you didn't tail-gate," I tell him, "and if you drove about ten miles an hour slower, you wouldn't have to wait for lights. These lights are phased for thirty miles per hour."

"I can read," Roy says.

We drive without speaking for about five minutes, and then Roy says, "Ace, have you always been an oddball? Earlene tells some awful strange stories about when you were a kid."

"I was a normal child," I say, "although somewhat impetuous, and inclined even as a youngster to clown around a bit."

Roy nods. "I can tell. It shows all over. You've always been a clown. Still are. And it's not funny."

"Virtually the only role left for an intellectual in our society," I say, "is that of clown."

"I wish you could forget that intellectual bit," Roy says. "You're a pretty decent fellow, sometimes, when you forget that you're smarter than God."

"And Marx."

"Never mind," Roy says. "I'm just playing along with the whole capitalistic game, if you know what I mean. Marx had the right idea. History will vindicate him."

He savors the word, and almost breaks out in a smile. If he weren't so addlepated, he would be dangerous. But then, this is probably true of all of us. (Including thyself, Oh Asa!)

"What women want," Roy says, "is a crude stud. Kind of dumb, but masculine and full of animal grace."

"Is this what Earlene saw in you?" I ask, genuinely dismayed at the implications of my brother-in-law's premise.

Before he can answer, Roy's foot jams the brake pedal, and the car glides into a little grocery truck ahead, smacking it a heavy, solid jolt. We both nod forward with the impact, and then sit there for a few seconds gathering in an impression of what's happened.

"Son of a bitch," Roy says.

The driver of the truck climbs out and walks back. Roy gets out of the car and says, "Sorry about that. Any damage?"

The two of them go to investigate, while Asa Bean dozes the seconds away in a nimbus of wrath, frustration, acedia and malaise. The clock in the dashboard glows faintly in the darkness of the car. The second hand sweeps sedately past the four,

101

the five and the six, and then the car starts to rock up and down from the efforts of Roy and his new-found acquaintance to dislodge their bumpers.

25

Several days pass.

With a surge of un-Beansian authority, Captain Asab—the mad captain of my soul—has launched forth out of the night that covers me, dark as the Pit from pole to pole, once more upon the quest of my sweet white mountainous and truly victorious (*vera nike*) whale. Moby Denise.

I divine the inner truth.

I probe, palpate.

Haruspex, with a harpoon. I crave the harpoonable harpoontang.

Or, Don Quixote Bean, the mad old doer (stung into frenzies of action), now waves the red flag of his ardor before the field of passion in the ring, and performs splendid Veronicas of terpsichorean lust, while the vast crowds lining the shimmering avenues of summer skies cry out, "Olé! Olé!"

Oh, Lay!

No. Caution be with thee, Asa.

More germanely, you are fulfilling a less direct destiny, resembling that great mythic Uncle, Judge Roy Bean, worshipping impossible Lily Langtrys in the barenness of his voyeur (Pecos) solitude.

Oh, the solitude of your saloon, where you judge your life and its deception, and where, with each passing hour, you measure the distance between that frontier impoverishment and the argosy of flesh contained in that twice-beloved, twin-hipped, geminating, bifurcating Venus Erotica, thy titological Veronica, Dyad deep in the mountains of your carmine lust, Oh Bean!

Which is all to say, I have phoned that Presence, and by various cunning codes, have determined that my passage to Cythera is barred by no embolus, either of fabrication or reluctance. Not only that, the mad father will be absent, selling class rings to high schools in impossibly distant regions.

Strike while the ikon is hot!

Veronica has consented to a date for this evening. I shall make her giggle once more, shattering that mask of cold beauty with the splendor of my assault. Fear not. Hesitate not. Trust and Assault, the very essence of the tale.

Feint heart ne'er won fair maiden. Be direct. Do not intellectualize.

Now I am walking to her apartment. Durango is using his Mustang to visit Sylvia Stevens. Durango the Satyr, horsing in that woodland.

Careful, Asa: your manic leaps will undo you, as they did your great grandfather, to the 60th power, Icarus Bean.

Be cool.

I stop at a neighborhood tavern, for I am an hour early. I need a drink, and order a double Bushmill's—a Hibernian fire to warm a Hibernal night.

The television set is blurring an evening news program, and there are three Charleys sitting at the bar, their heads turned in catatonic fixity toward the set. Videotropic heads.

I cast a random blessing outward into the night, hoping it might light upon the innocent fabulotropic head of my little niece, Debra.

But this is cowardice. It is cowardly to project our own moral responsibility to be joyful upon another. Therefore, I hope you will be as happy as I, Debra. And therefore I must be happy for my blessing to have meaning.

Asa Bean sits and drinks two quick ones, his hands cold from anxiety and ice-filled glasses.

Then, impetuously changing the pace, he drinks a Jim Beam and water.

He leaves the bar, and stops once more, half a block away, to buy a bottle of the afore-mentioned Jim Beam. (Nowhere can he fully escape the magic hint of his name.)

Once more he is walking in the darkness, feeling the cold wind flick fecklessly against his burning skin.

Veronica's apartment house now rocks silently into sight, tottering rhythmically with each Beamish boyish step of the lecherous Asa.

He climbs the familiar stairs, catches a brief hallucinatory glimpse of Jim Talbot missing the ball upon some celestial tee in the Heavens.

Thy Father, Oh Veronica!

Asa knocks, and the door is opened.

Blessed Veronica stands there, her eyes are shadowed (a startling circle of cyanosis about each luminous orb), and her pale skin glistens. Her hair glistens. Her hands glisten. Her sweetly exposed bosom glistens in marvelous cleavage, symmetrical with the glorious cleavage beneath, and Asa drifts in, at a loss for words.

What a loss is this!

Our embarrassment grows like a great balloon being inflated.

I cannot look at her.

I cannot speak.

Suddenly, I thrust the bottle of Jim Beam at her, and start talking about the only thing I can think of at the moment: the Sapir/Whorf hypothesis.

104

The more I talk, the more confused she becomes. The more confused she becomes, the more I talk.

We are caught in a terrible vortex.

She asks if I want a drink, and I machine-gun an answer to her, explaining why the Hopi Indians can't see the color orange, as Whorf explained.

"You see, it's a matter of linguistic programming," I say.

"What's that?" she asks. She seems afraid, suddenly. Poor girl, my heart goes out to her.

"Words," I say. "We are programmed by means of words. It's ironic, isn't it? We even *screw* by words!"

The obscenity, being the first between us, falls like a bowling ball to the floor at our feet. Veronica pats her hair nervously, her eyes going wild.

Don't panic, Asa! Don't panic.

But what this warning means is: PANIC, FOR CHRIST'S SAKE, PANIC!

I'm off again.

I am telling a visibly numb Veronica about a great-uncle of mine who was a prize fighter.

"He was called 'Kid Bean,'" I shouted. (My voice has been rising all along; I admit it.)

She arcs a look at me, gauging the distance and the wind.

But I will not be stopped.

"He was called 'Kid Bean,'" I repeat. "Actually, his full name was 'Kidney.' I mean, that was his *nickname,* not his full name. You know, as a kid. All the kids called him 'Kidney.' Isn't that just like kids?"

Veronica nods.

"So when he became a boxer, they called him 'Kid Bean,' you get it?"

Veronica nods again.

"Anyway, my great-uncle was *really* punch-drunk in his

later years. Let me tell you something, he was so goddam punch-drunk that when his wife wanted to get him up in the mornings, she had to count to nine."

Veronica takes a little sip of her drink.

"One morning, she counted to nine three times before he came around and got up on his knees. Right there on the bed; he'd get up on his knees and shake his head. Yes sir, my father's uncle. He was really knocked out that morning."

Veronica takes another tiny sip, and when she takes the glass away, she gives a little sob.

Now I am starting on something else, talking even faster and making even less sense. The poor girl wavers and her eyes glaze over.

This garrulity is suddenly, bewilderingly followed by a traumatic silence, a kind of lockjaw that twists my face, my head, my brain into an awesome contortion of dismayed paralysis.

I manage to open my mouth, and pour the whiskey down my throat.

I am suddenly blind, but I hear Veronica offering to refill my glass.

I agree.

I drink this, too.

Something is said, distantly.

It is my own, my very own voice, speaking of the way I used to catch tadpoles when I was a child.

I drink again.

I am drunk.

I leave the house, lurching and mumbling blasphemies. Masochist. Fool. Idiot. Crying, stupid Romantic. Hard-up clown. Imbecile. Cretin.

Veronica, your majestic ass was too important, too glorious for me to want to plumb it and descry the deficiencies of fact!

Sophist. Liar. King of liars. King Liar.

Drunken Asa M. Bean wanders upon the midnight streets, mumbling slogans and apophthegms, while an angry Veronica undoubtedly dances her slow, tired, sad way to bed and to sleep, appalled (as women must always be) at the astronomical, fascinating, infinitely exasperating folly of men.

26

Two days pass. Three days.

Deep in the warehouse, the faint morning light rests like a celestial powder upon the towering stacks of produce. I have not turned the section lights on yet, but I can see well enough to load eight crates of oranges on my pallet. My faithful bug idles behind and to the side of me. (It crops grass as Asa Bean sizes up the landscape amidst the citrus herd. . . . Great-grandson or great-grandnephew, or some perhaps more tenuous relationship, of Judge Roy Bean, from Vinegaroon, who held high court in an old saloon . . . and for a knifing or a shooting or any such fracas, Judge Bean was the law out west of the Pecos.)

He mounts the bug again, and merges once more into the mysterious dyad: centaur, cowboy, dreamer and cunning inhabitant of days and nights.

Before I can start it, Wilbur walks by on an aisle some forty feet away. He stops, reverses, and takes a long look down into the darkness.

"Hey, Soy Bean," he yells. "Is that you?"

"*C'est moi.*"

"What?"

"It's me."

"What you doing down there, man?"

"Getting eight crates of oranges for number twenty-two," I explain.

"How's come you don't turn on the lights, for Christ sake?"

"I'm finished," I say. "Only eight crates. I don't need lights for eight crates."

Wilbur walks on. At this instant, I am certain he is shaking his head slowly back and forth, awed by the eccentricity of Bean the Egghead.

At that instant I decide to send to Madge Hunter a list of essays I have planned to write. It is suddenly important for me to impress her with my intelligence.

I start to think of the list and almost run into a parked bug shortly before quitting time. Then, when we stop work fifteen minutes early, I am the first to finish washing up, and I go out to the order desk and tear off a sheet of paper. I look for a ballpoint pen, but can't find one. Durango comes up, and I see one in the pocket of his apron, and ask to borrow it from him.

"Sure," he says, and hands it to me.

I take it and start listing the titles of these hypothetical essays as follows:

"The Ironic Function of Deianira's Robe"
"The Irony of Kinship Roles Among the Ancient Celts"
"Ambiguities of Relevance: Studies in Time Focus"
"The Self-Bite of Satire"
"History as Invention and Fable"
"Language, the Source of Irony"

After I make the list, I stand there a few minutes admiring it. By God, any woman with warm blood in her brains would

108

admire a list like that. Such titles, I reflect, are better than any real essays could ever be.

Entelechy (Aristotle) has been oversold.

When I arrive home, I type up the list, and with sudden inspiration add another title: "Oedipus As Mock King."

Then I put it in an envelope, along with a cool and succinct note saying, "You might be interested in these essays I'm planning to write; and perhaps you can help me."

The lie is outrageous flattery, of course. Old Madge will be knocked off her round firm ass by the request.

I'm aware of one thing though: she is a shrewd broad, in spite of all her screwy ways. Distinctly, she is the kind who will be intrigued by the off-beat approach (such as receiving a list of essay titles in the mail).

The voice that assures me of these things sounds vaguely like Durango's.

And Durango knows.

Suddenly I am aware of the pen I have been using, and realize that it is the one I borrowed from Durango at the warehouse, and that I forgot to return to him.

But there is something else, something insidiously familiar that has been ironically teasing me (as if part of my brain refuses to recognize a fact of this voltage, this magnitude) all along as I have been using the damned thing.

I look at the ballpoint: it is totally, heartbreakingly familiar—the typical advertising pen (cost $8.50 a gross), made of diaphanous white plastic, and carrying the anonymous gray print on its shank. This one reads, "Altmeier Printing Company."

I read the legend, and then my mind starts to whirl, and I remember the Dürer mask, the blasphemous, drunken old pseudo-golfer, and Veronica's sweet voice, surprising giggle and plenitudinous ass. I remember the sad, stale-smelling little apartment and the inert mobile hanging in the dumb air.

God!

Durango knows, indeed!

27

I have been thinking about the ballpoint pen, and the more I think about it, the more it seems plausible to me that *I actually gave one to Durango*. Yes, now that I think of it, I surely gave him one.

Anyway, I can't find the extra ones. *Something* happened to the damned things.

At work, I watch Durango. I study his face, everything about it. The dark-circled eyes, the heavy blue-black beard that will never shave close (a chronic ecchymosis of the jaw and chin) . . . in a word, the sinister Mediterranean in all his flamboyant untrustworthiness. . . .

No, I school myself rapidly away from such thoughts. Durango is an innocent, beneath all the casual obscenities that spill out of his mouth. His deceits are clearly delineated and predictable. He is not a betrayer of friends. He is, when all is said and done, *advocatus fabuli*.

The ride home on the bus is like an ugly little nap with my eyes open.

I climb the steps to my bedroom.

Earlene is in the kitchen, doing something. I think she's cleaning out her cabinets. She can't be getting dinner this early. It's only ten after two.

Dazed and tired, I approach the door to my room, and I

think of Veronica's door, and wonder—for the sixtieth time—what she is thinking, what she is doing. Is it too late? Is it too late?

There is a chair in the hall, and on the chair I see a week-old newspaper that I have been looking at every day as I pass this place. I wonder vaguely what it is doing there, and then, without really thinking, I pick it up and take it into my bedroom, where I throw it on the bed.

I am suddenly too tired even to start my tub, so I sit on the bed and look through the paper, and something I see there makes me stop. It is an announcement that there will be a Rubens exhibit at the art museum, starting next Thursday, and the exhibit will be for two weeks.

Rubens.

The slot-machine handle cranks, the wheels grind in a deep nickel rhonchus, and one, two, three breast-warm plums jump into sight at the windows.

Suddenly, my mind is filled with great shoals of naked women. Thick-waisted, plump-titted, stocky-legged nymphs are thundering down the dormitory hallways of my imagination, and with a sigh I throw the paper aside and lie back on my bed.

I am aware that I can go to sleep, right now, without my bath. I can bathe when I wake up. No difference.

But before I go to sleep, the Anarchist, the Shawnee and the Assassin come out and stand waiting. The Assassin is picking his nose. All are expectant.

Of course. We all know what we want.

There is too much recognition in this discovery, and it does not even come close to keeping me awake.

But already, it seems, my mind is made up. My plans are cast. And I have only until next Wednesday to prepare Durango and Veronica Talbot for the grand duteous act.

28

Asa Bean awakes, groggy with late-afternoon sleep, and takes his bath. Lying on his back in the tub, with his beard floating before him, he experiences a pantheistic dream, in which he is turning slowly into seaweed and kelp, and small birds pick their way through the salt marshes of his capacious love.

Poseidon, meditating upon a distant thalassic field, flowering with foam like the myriad blossoms in a meadow of white clover. Or Nereus, sire of fifty daughters fated to fecundate all rivers, lakes, ponds, waterfalls, tides, seas, oceans, bays and swamps.

Asa Bean yearns to become a myth, as we all do, and transcend the A & P Warehouse, 1526 Marlborough Heights and the inscrutable dialectics of his foolish and bewildering existence. This myth is manifold, subtle and changing. In trying to become this myth, Asa Bean is trying to find himselves.

I arise from the tub, streaming tepid water from my shoulders, arms, crotch and thighs. My beard is matted warmly to my chin and throat. I dry myself in a frenzy of gesticulations, rub a little hair tonic in my hair and beard and put on my snow-white terry-cloth robe.

Like Odysseus, risen from the waters, I stride as proudly (and metaphoramiscibly) as a scented prince into my bedroom, and there is my ubiquitous niece, Debra, sitting on the floor and playing with my shoe laces.

"What sort of Nausicaä is this?" I ask, in a giant's voice.

Debra lifts her gaze, smiling dreamily at the game that exists between us.

I shoo her out of my laces and out of the room, and dress myself thoughtfully. Then I go downstairs, and commence to work on the Deianira thing. I am thinking of the dimensions of this myth. There is something I want to communicate to Madge Hunter, and I want to get it clear in my mind first. There are a million messages from the past, and it is good for all Mankind—I say to myself—that there is an occasional fun-loving irrelevancy, like Asa Bean, to decode these messages.

All afternoon I work on the problem of the symbolic robe, and manage to type it up in readable form.

Roy comes home, angry and morose, for the apartment-building sale fell through. He is hurt, bewildered, shamed. He thinks the world is pointing a finger at him, and scorning him in his fecklessness. To be a valid Marxist, Roy understands, one must first prove that he understands, and can cope with, capitalistic mysticism.

He goes up to his room, where I suspect he is occupying himself momentarily by leafing through old familiar scatological works, to sustain him in his travail.

I go out into the kitchen, and Earlene says, "Asa, I talked with Madge today, and she got your letter."

"She did?"

"Yes, and she says she found it enormously interesting. Do you know something?"

"What?"

"She noticed something."

"What?"

"She noticed something that I've noticed for years, except I've never really noticed it." She pauses, frowns; even Earlene is intimidated by such a clot of unintentional equivocation.

"What I mean is, I've never really been *aware* of it, until Madge mentioned it."

I open the fridge, stare at the cans of beer all lined in a row, and then change my mind and close the door.

"Well, aren't you going to ask what it is?"

"Sure. What is it?"

"You're ironic. All the essay titles were ironic, Madge noticed. Not only that, it's written all over you. And Madge says that irony is a man's invention. Women are never ironic."

"Women are never ironic!" I mimic her in a nasty voice.

"Well, it's true."

"Women are so goddam perfect, they make me want to puke."

"Never mind, they're not ironic."

"Of course not. Not if it's *bad*."

"Well, they're not."

"I guess not. Okay, okay. It's a man's invention. It's ironic, though, that most of our ironies have to do with women."

"What is *that* supposed to mean?"

"I have no idea," I said.

She chewed on that for a while, and then she said, "Asa, did I tell you that we've gotten our demonstration all planned? Listen, this is really going to be something! People around this city will really know about FORCE when this is all over."

I pull a Miller's High Life out and pop the top. A little cold froth sprays my hand, and I drink the coldness, feeling it coil down my throat—a long chilly, fizzy dangle of beer, beginning already to twirl in the peristalsis of hunger that is now known to be Essence of A. Bean.

"I'll let you in on something, if you promise you won't tell," Earlene says. She has just put a casserole in the oven, and she is standing facing me with a potholder in each hand.

114

I raise my eyebrows, without answering, but that is enough. Earlene throws the potholders on the counter beside the sink, and says, "It's going to be Wednesday. That's all I can tell you. Where and what are going to remain secrets. Only the women on the board know about that. Even the members are going to be in the dark until Wednesday."

"It sounds exciting," I say, trying to sound convinced.

"Madge is working day and night," Earlene says. "She asks about you, though. You know something? She really seems to like you. Why don't you give her a ring?" Earlene laughs. "I mean on the telephone, of course. At least for the present."

I am a little surprised, because I have been thinking of getting the Deianira article to her. But, of course, Earlene's overtness causes me to pull in my horns.

"I'll tell you one thing," Earlene says, "Madge is a really sweet and reasonable person. She's not the gold digger a lot of women are. I mean, you wouldn't even have to take her out. She's said a thousand times that one way women have to emancipate themselves is to stop acting the part of the recipient, the passive, brainless receiver of things brought to them by men."

"What you mean," I say, "is that Madge wouldn't mind going Dutch treat."

"Exactly," Earlene says. "Exactly."

"You know," I say, "I've always wondered what the poor Dutch ever did to deserve that nasty bit of antonomasia."

"What?"

"You know, having it called 'Dutch treat.' Why not *French* treat? Or *Spanish* treat?"

"Asa," Earlene says, "will you please stop spiraling off with words? You know, language is to *use,* not to think about all the time."

115

"Let me get that down on paper," I say, looking all around, as if for a pen and note pad.

"Oh shut up," Earlene says. "And please get back to the subject."

"Which is?"

"Which is you and Madge."

"If she's so big on this egalitarian thing between the sexes," I say, "why doesn't she call me up and invite me to dinner? I'd be helpless, and she could probably have her way with me. Passionately."

"She just may," Earlene says. "Only, there's no reason *you* can't make the first move. I mean, Madge has *feelings,* and she doesn't want to call you up unless there's some . . . you know, some . . . tangible sign you like her, too."

"Hmmm," I say. Then I nod and repeat the hum.

Earlene clasps her forehead dramatically, falls back against the counter, and cries, "You mean, I'm actually getting *through* to you? You mean, my brother Asa is actually paying *attention* to something his dumb sister *said?*"

"Don't be sarcastic," I say. "Leave that to your betters-in-wit."

Roy appears at the door in his skivvies, and says, "Somebody call my name?"

"I said 'wit,' " I tell him. "Not 'shit.' "

"Thanks a lot," Roy says, reaching into the fridge for a beer.

"Honestly," Earlene says, "one of these days, you two are going to float away on a stream of beer."

"Oh that reminds me," Earlene says, clasping her head in her hands to calm herself down.

"What reminds you of what?" Roy asks.

"There was a phone call for Asa. Some man. He wanted you to play golf."

"Play *golf!*" Roy exclaims, turning his slow gaze upon me, as if challenging me to explain the enormity of this foolishness.

Earlene gives several little swift nods at the wall and looks sure of herself. "That's what he said," she says. "That's *exactly* what he said. Golf."

"In *this* kind of weather?" Roy asks, outraged.

"I only took the message," Earlene explains reasonably.

Roy takes a long therapeutic sip from his beer, and says, "Ace, you sure know some wiggly people."

Earlene frowns and concentrates. "Let me see, his name was Talbot. I've got it down on the note pad by the telephone. Jim Talbot."

"I know," I say.

"He didn't say whether you should call back or not."

"I don't think I will."

"*I* sure wouldn't," Roy says.

"He didn't talk very clearly," Earlene says. "Do you suppose he was drunk or something?"

"I suspect that is possible," I say.

"Yes sir," Roy says, "some really wiggly, wiggly people."

Including yourself, Brother-in-Law Scobie, standing there in your skivvies and socks, pontificating upon normality.

Including your wife.

Including Ahasucrus M. Bean, the Wandering Methodist and Champion of Persiflage and Intellectual Trickery.

29

Earlene's talk about the mysterious forthcoming demonstration made me forget the Deianira article. And strange to say, it made me forget about Madge Hunter (at least, for the time being, and as a sex object).

In those few trips I had made into the art museum, even though I had carried the pearl-handled jackknife, I had not satisfied this dumb-ass urge I have.

I suppose it is a truism that everyone has absolute blind spots in his personality—attitudes or fixations that he cannot even remotely understand . . . isn't even sure exist, perhaps. As the smart fellow says: "I don't know who first discovered the ocean, but I know it wasn't a fish."

So here I am swimming around in my life, trying to find my selves (which includes trying to find my ocean, of course); and the one abiding thing, it seems, is this sense of standing before a beautiful and famous painting, and pulling out the pearl-handled knife. Do people really *love* such paintings? Would the world really be lessened if they were *all* destroyed (let alone just one from a traveling exhibit)?

Evanescence and vulnerability are the prerequisites of value. (Asa Bean, the Aphorist.)

A few of my selves come to visit me periodically. There are, of course, the well-known acronymic Anarchist, Shawnee and Assassin. But these are visible precisely insofar as they are not as intimate as others. They are less dominant (or less essential?) to my populations than the dark citizenry who permanently attend the dark councils of my dark motivations.

118

I do not know what mysterious votes were taken, what caucuses and secret meetings were held, what deals were made over booze in the smoky hotel suites of my intentions; but obviously something would not be right until I made this climactic trip to the art museum, and confronted a Rubens nude (female) with my pearl-handled knife opened (male) and stood there in an absolutely simple and apocalyptic moment, discovering something about myself (male) and woman (female) and art (male) and beauty (female) and Man.

At least I would never know until it happened. And the announcement of the Rubens opening was too much to ignore. Was it possible that I secretly hated women, and this was the reason for my excitement? All the exasperated assemblies in all my chambers arose in a body, and with catcalls, hisses, cries of outrage and ridicule, gave the lie to this surmise . . . but Freud (half-baked, half-fried, half-fraud) taught us to be wary, and to believe that for every visible chamber in our awareness, there is a dark counter-chamber in the unconscious, whose vote more often than not runs in opposition to the other. The only distinction is: how many *belong* to this legislative and governing body in the subconscious, and what is their strength in the last analysis?

One way to tolerate the mad beast we live inside is to feed it, ambiguously indulge it, never cease trying to understand it, and occasionally give it something to do. Whole empires have been destroyed upon this principle, but the principle lives on, and conceivably, on occasion, does good and evil indifferently.

Today I borrowed forty dollars from Roy.

30

The weather has turned warm. The temperature is hovering near thirty degrees, and the streets have been rubbed bare by the traffic.

Earlene is hanging new flowered drapes with satin linings in the front room. Roy (fully dressed, for he has to stand in the window now and then) is helping her. She is excited. Something nest-building (female) in her is turned on loud, and her eyes are shining and her voice is constantly on the verge of spilling over.

No man is guilty until proved innocent. What I mean is, no man is innocent until proved guilty. What I really mean is, I must not, for sweet sanity's sake, judge Durango on the basis of that circumstantial Altmeier Printing Company ballpoint pen.

And of course I have really convinced myself that I gave him one. Early in life, I learned to give in a spirit of self-hypnosis, so that I would not gloat upon my goodness later. I felt this was the only way to give (for I did want to be moral), and of course it is; however, it is unfortunate in such circumstances as this that I can't fully recover the episode of handing the pen over to Durango. I envision it ("Here, Durango: something you might use"—this in various geographical points of the warehouse) . . . but they all evaporate before the lens of my imagination.

No matter. I will trust them both. I will trust Durango and I will trust Veronica. Justice is, after all, an act of will. As is charity.

120

So I pick up the telephone and dial the possibly perfidious Durango's number. He answers.

"This is Soy Bean," I say.

"How are you?" On the phone, Durango talks primly, as if for posterity.

"Listen," I say, my voice getting a little lower. "You remember when I told you about my plan? You know, with the paintings?"

An instant's silence. Then a noncommittal, "Yeah, I remember."

"Well, I want to talk to you after work tomorrow. At The Fifth Wheel. Veronica too. I want her in on it too."

"What you mean, 'in on it'?" Durango asks.

"Never mind. I'll explain things tomorrow. I just didn't want you making other plans."

"Well," Durango says, "I'll listen. Won' hurt nothin going to The Fifth Wheel, I guess. I can always drink a beer."

"Sure," I say. Adaptable Durango. "It's a deal, then. Okay?"

"I guess so," Durango says.

We hang up, and then I look up Veronica's number. I dial it, but the phone rings busy. I pace around the house a little, watch Roy and Earlene with the drapes, and then return to the phone.

This time, the phone rings, and Veronica answers.

"How about having a beer with me after work tomorrow afternoon," I say.

"Sure. I guess so."

"I want to tell you about a plan of mine," I say. "It won't take long. Afterward, I want you and Durango to come with me."

"Where to?" she asks.

"Well, it's an art museum."

121

"A *what?*"

"An art museum. I'll explain it all tomorrow afternoon."

"What are you going to do in a place like *that?*"

"I'll explain it all, like I said."

"But why do you want *me* to come?"

"Tomorrow. . . ."

"I know," she interrupts. "Tomorrow afternoon. You certainly do seem to get some funny ideas, Asa," she says.

Her using my name like that makes me feel good. I think her tone was warm, intimate. Veronica amused/disturbed by Asa's antics.

We hang up, and then I go into the front room, where Earlene and Roy stand back and ask me how I like the new drapes.

I tell them fine, but I am thinking of the museum, and I am deeply excited by the thought of what we will be doing tomorrow, after we leave The Fifth Wheel.

31

I have been drinking beer, waiting for Veronica to get off work. She herself has served me, and every time she comes up I pat her leg under the table. She doesn't move away, and sometimes even drops a smile upon me. The Dürer mask is warm, and I am certain she is interested in my plan. She is curious. As men, we owe this to women: to get crazy ideas that occupy us, as devils once occupied imaginative men in the Middle Ages, and drive us a little wicked or mad. Women don't know this, but they understand it well. It is a subcutaneous truth for them.

Women cerebrate with their ovaries, analyze with their mammaries. Their reality grasp is awesome, and their gift for feeling, miraculous. Their feelings constitute a philosophy—rich, subtle, intricate. These feelings outplay our masculine fever to rationalize (*cacoëthes rationis,* upon the chessboard, until we realize that it might be the wrong board, and that the game might even not be chess).

It is almost five o'clock, quitting time for Veronica, when she will throw aside her apron, tidy up her hair and come over to join Durango and me in the booth; where I will reveal my plan.

In a blink of time, she is doing precisely as I previsioned, and with equal miraculousness, Durango is now standing by the booth. He slides in the other side. Veronica presses her abundance against my hip, as if in response to the sudden constriction in the booth.

She is a sensitive woman. How could I have doubted her? All hail.

Now I am letting my idea slither out (slop out, like warm guts spilling from a slit peritoneum) upon the table before the two of them. They are silent, Veronica's eyes are clouded, her hip no longer touching mine.

She smokes a cigarette, the Dürer mask a little colder than I seem to remember.

I am saying all kinds of crazy-ass things . . . things I don't even believe. Never *have* believed. I keep talking about this as a work of art. The Supremely Gratuitous (I explain what the word means).

All of the sins of the dadaists, all of the sins of two centuries of goliards, all of the sins of dervishes, madmen, sha-

123

mans (the Shawnee nods and bathes his fingers in rabbit blood), surrealists, Dionysians, juju pilgrims and devils . . . all these sins, vibrant as ideational seeds in their exotic linguistic pods, burst forth and flower in this tiny desert of the commonplace. The Fifth Wheel.

Durango's eyes are a little off to the side. He lights a small Antonio & Cleopatra cigar, no bigger than half a lead pencil.

I grab Durango's wrist and shake his arm. I lean forward and hiss: "Aren't you just about fed up, Durango?"

"What you mean, 'fed up?'" he asks warily.

"All this goddam talk," I say. "That's all there is, talk, talk, talk. The whole world is falling apart, man, and what do we do? We sit here talking. I mean, it's about time we *do* something. Look around you. Read the papers. Listen to the radio. And what are *we* doing? Sitting here in The Fifth Wheel, drinking beer and *talking*."

Durango casts a contemplative look in the distance and says, "No offense intended, Soy Bean, but as a matter of fact, seems to me *you* the one that's doin all the talkin."

"Listen," I say, "that's not the point. The point is, if you don't get out and *do* something, for God's sake, you're not even *alive*."

"Hell, I'm alive," Durango says.

"Action's the thing, Durango. Action. Believe me: I'm an authority on this. All my life I've been spinning my wheels, and I've finally come to the realization that I've got to get out and *do* something. The old beast-in-the-jungle syndrome. I mean, I'm not asking you and Veronica to do anything: I'll do *everything*. I just want you to come along, and share in it. I mean, what are friends for?"

The statement surprises me a little, and I suddenly realize that Asa needs friends. It's that simple. Why should he be any different? But the fact is, I don't often think of him this way.

124

Underneath all his dodges, persiflage, confabulation and verbal sortilege, the poor fool wants to build bridges to others and form a sodality of peers. Isobean.

"How about it?" I ask. "Can't you feel the excitement of it? Don't you realize what freedom is? How many people could witness something like this, graced as it is by the fully articulated, fully premised joy of impulse? How about it?"

Durango looks uncomfortable, vaguely troubled.

Suddenly, my life passes before me in a flash. When I talk against talk, I am talking. And of course, talk is my thing, my bag. Talk is my genesis. God said, "Let there be light" (proving himself the Archetypal Poet, for he spoke realities into being), and then he said, "Let there be Beans." This was sometime after the first day, of course; but contingent upon that, for beans grow only in knowledge.

Undoubtedly, I am still spinning my wheels. All but the Fifth Wheel, for the sedate atmosphere lies upon me like a cloud of comfortable apathy.

I am ready to shout, but instead—with admirable control— I repeat my question to both of them: "How about it?"

Simultaneously, Durango and Veronica take long drinks from their glasses.

"Well?" I repeat, "Are you interested in coming with me?"

Veronica draws a tidy circle of wetness on the table before her. A raveling of Durango's cigarette smoke stings my eye, and dissipates.

Veronica takes a breath and says, "Well, it all sounds kind of interesting, from what I can understand. But Asa, I still don't understand why you're doing it."

"That's the living mystery that is at the heart of everything," I say. "*All* our motivations, when you analyze them. Why do we do *anything?* Isn't there an ultimate, totally free action? Isn't there beauty in such a thought?" Suddenly, I am overwhelmed by the asininity of what I am saying.

And I see the two of them aligned against me in dark complicity.

"Soy Bean," Durango says, "you too much for us, man. Why don' you get some intellectuals you can talk to? Maybe they understand what you saying, but we sure as hell don'."

"It isn't that I'm not *interested,*" Veronica says, possibly (I think) frowning with the effort of dissociating herself from Durango's "we," and articulating a shadowy thought, "but I just don't *understand!*"

Maybe I'm just drunk on the beer. But suddenly I am exasperated. Something pops in my head, and goes whizzing around the room like a crazy model airplane, overcharged with high-octane fuel.

Then it occurs to me: Veronica has just put herself down. She is sitting there, tired, discouraged, bored with the familiar faces and landscape of The Fifth Wheel, and trying to be polite to me. The poor girl . . . working in a place like this, with a colossal windbag and tosspot of a father to support. Maybe she likes me; maybe she simply has a warm compassion for anybody as obviously screwed-up as I am.

But why doesn't she giggle?

"Listen," I say, a tremor of passion in my voice as I clasp the back of her hand that is resting on the table. "Listen, a woman needs a brain about as much as she needs a third tit."

Durango looks shocked. (Durango is sensitive about strong language? The thought, as Adlai Stevenson would have said, staggers the imagination!)

Neither of them understands.

Suddenly, another little model airplane takes off, and I am sitting there talking about fifty different things, and not making any sense at all. Not only am I drunk, but I am feverish. I

126

distinctly remember having a sore throat this morning. Or maybe yesterday morning. Raskolnikov, the diseased giant, turns into a sickly colony of gnats whispering upon a dead arm, or a school of carp wallowing feverishly in celestial mud.

A man can stand only so much.

Suddenly I stand up and stride out of The Fifth Wheel, my head whirring. The landing field tilts under the malevolent stars.

I myself am the model airplanes. Both of me. It is I who have flown away, and now drunkenly circle the airfield, where Poor Veronica and Stout Durango sit watching my stunts. (Faithful, I swear! How could I have doubted them?) I am once more in search of myselves.

The situation has undergone a sudden, catastrophic entropy.

My lambent, demi-urgic energies have spread all over the landscape, and outside I possess the illusion of warmth in the greater, more relevant illusion of eighteen-degree weather.

For an instant, as I pace swiftly down the road, I think I hear Durango calling, "Hey, Soy Bean," but I'm not sure.

Suddenly a bus swerves over and wheezes her breezy doors open.

Sweet Whore that takes on all passengers for money, the bus now glides out upon the road, with her most faithful customer, Asa Bean, the Despondent Sentimentalist.

I am alone in the world, and there is a comfort in that. Sometimes. But not now.

Entropy.

The city glides past, winking at me with a thousand variegated lights. It is dark already. Six o'clock.

The world is turning over in its human sleep, and Asa Bean speeds outward, exploded by oceanic confusions, pestilential need and his own intransigent comicity.

32

I am standing beside the statue of Boadicea and her hounds in front of the building. Behind me, there are twenty steps; before me, there are nine. Let it be said: I am on the side of Boadicea.

I stand on the twenty-first step, and go up on my toes, flexing the gastrocnemius muscles in the backs of my legs. I can see the top half of my body in the massive glass doors ahead. I am wearing my red ski cap and a U.S. Navy pea coat that I bought at a discount store four and a half months ago. I see before me the upper half of a bearded man, looking a little like Starbuck (I think), or maybe it's Stubb. Anyway, he could be one of the *Pequod*'s crew. I like this fantasy. (I think it's Stubb.)

Fanfare of silence.

The same dumpy little guard, dressed in a blue uniform (the exact color of my pea coat), rests his tired, familiar, ancient eyes upon me as I walk past. The weight of his vision is almost imperceptible, but I am aware that he is regarding me.

I walk past, climbing more steps as I approach the foyer that connects the front display chambers. Marble all about me, great livid columns holding up a dull lavender paisley ceiling some thirty feet overhead. My steps resound in the great chamber.

Contempt. Only a scattering of people here to view the opening. All of those plump luscious broads spread out upon rich canvases inside, and only these few people—overdressed and undereducated. Whispering to give the impression of dignity to the occasion and/or themselves.

Asa Bean, at an apocalyptic juncture in his chronic search for himselves. He called in sick today, not being up to facing Durango and the warehouse gang.

I walk forward into the first viewing room, noticing everything about me. A trickle of dirty string on the marble floor, next to the wall. A single, silver gum wrapper, balled up the size of a ruptured marble, and lying in the center. Will my foot touch it? I increase my stride slightly, and step upon it.

A dozen people are in the first display chamber. The great paintings, the large glossy two-dimensional slabs of flesh, slap me brightly in the face as I enter. My hand clasps the closed pearl-handled knife until the both of them compose a single bulge of sweating knuckled meat.

Slowly I pace forward, "The Portrait of an Old Man" on my left, and "The Rape of the Daughters of Leucippus" on my right. I veer to the right, and stand ten feet in front of the painting, hands in my pockets, eyes half-closed. Briefly, I look about me.

There are six or seven people in the room—two groups, one consisting of three middle-aged ladies, and another of two women and a tall, stooped man with a dignified expression.

Then another man—a loner, like myself—comes in, and walks down the other wall, hands behind his back.

My pulse is suddenly galloping away, and I am aware of something critical happening. I move on down the line to the next painting, which is unfamiliar to me, and for some reason Asa Bean, the Usually Compulsive Verbalist, doesn't even bother to read the title.

The painting shows a naked woman, full-face, eating grapes and holding the bunch in both hands. Her coy little titties (larger, sweeter grapes) are peeking out from the crooks of her arms. One knee is raised, concealing her victorious triangle, and staring brainlessly (as knees must) and boldly out upon the observer.

Vaguely classical, vaguely pretty, vaguely familiar (I think vaguely of Veronica), the picture moves me strangely. The hand in my right pocket aches like a diseased tooth. My head is hot, feels stuffed with oyster dressing.

Part of the glory will be if I do it with all these people around. The thought of consequences shrinks to the view through a small, irrelevant keyhole, in which I can see a future no larger or more important than the interior of a cigar box.

The woman in the painting is staring at me. I am trying to make out her expression. There is a sound of agitation deep inside my mind, the milling of a crowd of confusion rumbling aimlessly down the corridors of my sensorium.

I've got to jar that bitch's stare! She's too self-possessed, too smug to exist like that!

A sort of fury gallops through me, wild horses and a shower of leaves pulverizing the air. All my lakes and ponds ripple from the force. The sounds of agitation increase. I seem to tilt vertiginously, awed by the power of this painted woman gazing back at me, the bunch of grapes eternally poised beside her little rosebud lips. Like the fox, she will bite into them with her premolars, and as in the old superstition, I must bite into this vixen's heart and taste it, or I will never be wise.

I am flapping like a flag in a cyclone. Great flocks of pigeons (old symbols of lasciviousness) flutter in my eyes and in the bulging sacks of my arms and legs. There are shouts . . . women's voices crying out, and then a sort of song with female voices. They sound like all girls, all girlhood, singing . . . the Campfire Girls, chanting:

130

Rachel, Rachel, I've been a thinking
What a wonderful world this would be,
If all the baw-eeze were transported
Far across the azure sea.

It can't really be that song can it? I am transfixed, not transported, by the hallucinatory power of the moment.

This is it.

This painted, lovely Siren (*Un concetto di bellézza!*), with soft and cunning ferrets, minks and doves nesting together in her bosom, has lured me to this point, and now dares me to slice her icon withershins, revealing the lost moon of beauty.

I remove the knife, swooning with the ecstasy of this most epiphanic event: I flip open the long, sharp blade that wobbles in its sheath. Suddenly, a score of cicatrices, a score of scorings jump into focus, over her breasts and arms and warm loose belly.

This is how she will look, after the rape of Asa M. Bean.

I tilt again, and little electric engines are humming in my head. Ménière's syndrome? Psychogenic syncope?

We are living on the year hand of an enormous clock, and we turn too slowly for the naked eye to catch.

Then I discover the depths of my depravity: before I slice this innocent sacrificial whore, I will have to do the symbolically appropriate thing—I will have to expose myself.

She must understand one aspect of the ceremonial nature of this confrontation.

Horrified at the thought, I nevertheless experience a hideously realistic scene (Do I? Don't I?). The film shakes, gives off phosphorescent flakes, and the Anarchist (now the Ancient Mariner) scurries down a rat hole . . . I fancy, in a surge of sodium pentothal clarity, that I unzip my pants and am about to release that strong and brutal implement that has tyrannized over my life for so long, when there is a sudden jolt of sound at the entrance to the display chamber.

Asa Bean, the Pervert

Asa Bean, the Grotesque.

But have I *done* it? Fans whirr, the camera moves, the world turns.

Oh, veil!

Asa Bean, the hyper-imaginative, who will fancy a thousand sins for every sin he actually believes in enough to commit.

For isn't this why we have imaginations, to contemplate those things that are "too horrible to contemplate"? Of course. Of course! And that is why we have books and pictures, Age-old Bean, to relieve us of the obligation of actually *doing* certain things—the great dramas prevail beneath the literal—that must inevitably exercise an insidious appeal to at least a few of every man's selves.

Walter Pidgeon (old cinematic symbol of lust) understood this, when he stalked Hitler with his loaded rifle. It is the old dance between art (male) and life (female). We must always attempt it, always obey the caller's call. *Vive,* l'endeavored dance.

A sudden burst of sound at the door. Women singing. They are not mere data of my wild dream populations, but real warm, tumultuous, tumble-fleshed women coming through the door. Aghast, in imagination I zip up imaginary pants and turn to face them. The Rubens broad slips out of my mind, and sinks in the vortex behind me, a joyful whore's helix into Nirvana, anonymity, the past.

There are ten, fifteen, twenty women—nicely, properly dressed, many of them middle-aged (or verging upon it)— marching into the display room, singing:

132

Rubens, Rubens, I've been a thinking
What a wonderful world this would be,
If you men could respect us as persons
And liberate us from harlotry.

Finally there are twenty-five or thirty of them, crowded together at the entrance of the room. Quickly, they form three rows (the short women in front, the middle-sized in the middle and the tall ones in back), and they sing this verse over and over, about ten times.

Four of them are carrying signs. One sign reads:

> WE ARE NOT SEX OBJECTS
> WE ARE HUMAN BEINGS!

Another, carried by a woman who is obviously bra-less:

> WE'RE NO LONGER MOO COWS
> WE'VE PROGRESSED SINCE RUBENS' TIME

Another:

> WOMEN ARE TIRED OF BEING JUST
> PRETTY, PATIENT, AND UNDERSTANDING

And the last, which I like best of all, carried by a platinum-haired wench with bright, sassy eyes:

> FEE, FIE, FO, FUM,
> I'M TIRED OF BEING
> BLONDE AND DUMB

All of this takes place very quickly, of course, and during about the third or fourth rendering of the "Rubens" song, I see Earlene and Madge Hunter standing together in the second row.

Both are looking at me as they sing—Madge is grinning,

but Earlene looks a little troubled; undoubtedly she knows why I am here, and is afraid I might disrupt their disruption with some neurotic irrelevancy.

Finally, two guards come in (possibly to see that they don't rip up any paintings in an excess of muliebrity), and stand before the group, watching and listening with uncomfortable looks on their faces.

So far, the women haven't touched any of the paintings, but God knows what the future will hold, so I take the opportunity to sneak into the next room, through a small crowd that is accumulating to peer through at the demonstrators.

Immediately before leaving through the side entrance, I think I hear a surge of noise (alarums, imbroglio, the rapid whispering of "Rhubarb, rhubarb, rhubarb," by seedy mustachioed actors on a darkened stage).

Asa Bean, the elusive, compulsively reflective Vandal, escapes, his red ski cap flashing in the dark wintry light of afternoon, his pea coat a moving blot against the dirty detritus of old snow lining the walks.

His mind whirls with adjectives, adverbs, pronouns and verbs, all looking for a noun to rest in.

Once again he sets out . . . in search of himselves, but through these hoping to arrive at a vision of the holy Vale of Hypostasis.

Avail.

33

"Hey, Soy Bean!"
Deep in the forest gloom of the potato aisles, I sit and nurse

my hot coffee. A cold, relentless draft, smelling of undifferentiated vegetable, blows down the aisle, chilling my ankles and caressing my arms and neck. The four demonic birds of the modern apocalypse—Disappointment, Irony, Anger and Frustration—sit upon the girders under the skylights, and gaze down upon me out of bleary knowing eyes.

"Hey, Soy Bean!"

Durango's voice is closer. He smells my spoor. He is on the next aisle.

"Hey, why the fuck you hidin, man?"

Durango comes up and sits down beside me on the edge of a pallet. It is seven o'clock in the morning, coffee-break time. Linda Thorpe and the other office workers haven't even come in yet. Carbon fumes from the bugs still marble the dark air fanned by the cold breezes down the aisles.

Durango puts his coffee cup down and lights a cigarette. The smell is good as Durango exhales audibly and says, "Jesus H. Christ, it's cold in here this mornin."

Then he turns his head aside and yells, "Hey, Wilbur, turn up the fuckin heat!"

No answer. Durango's yells are part of the ecology of the warehouse before eight o'clock, like bird songs in the jungle.

"Hey, Soy Bean, I wan' talk to you, man."

"Okay," I say, dipping my face into my coffee, knowing what's coming, but not knowing how it's coming.

"Man, you were really drunk the other day! That why you called in sick yesterday?"

"I guess I was pretty crazy in there," I say.

"In The Fifth Wheel?" Durango asks. "Yeah, and the way you took off, all a sudden, like somebody built a fuckin fire about two feet up your ass-hole."

Picturesque speech and patter from Durango.

Asa Bean sips his coffee, nods, makes vaguely understand-

135

ing and agreeable noises and gestures. Phatic communion. Durango talks, smokes his cigarette and sips coffee, leisurely scattering obscenities with the largess of a Sicilian *bandito* chief.

"What did you do after I left?" I ask Durango.

He frowns, taps his cigarette ash on the toe of his shoe, and takes a big breath.

"Nothin," he says finally. The enormity of his lie is palpable, thick, odorous.

I get a brief glimpse of Veronica's heels dancing toward the ceiling, Durango, still in a turtle-neck shirt, rutting her with long vigorous charges.

"What do you mean, nothing?" I ask him.

Durango's frown gathers intensity. Becomes grotesque, excruciating. "Hey, Soy Bean, lemme ask you somethin, man."

"Ask away," I say, standing up. Maybe I'll kick him in the face while he's sitting there.

"You really *like* Veronica?"

I step over to Durango, and his head turns back as he keeps his look on me. For the first time in our friendship, I see something wary in his expression.

"You son of a bitch," I say, "did you get in her pants? Did I give you that pen?"

Durango jumps to his feet and cries, "Hell no! What you talkin about, Soy Bean? *What* pen?"

The enormity of my accusation leaves me weak. Clearly, I have betrayed Durango, who is (or has been) one of the few friends I've ever had. The realization laps over me, and I swallow and turn back, looking for my coffee.

"Man, you gotta watch that temper," Durango says. "You fly off the handle like a fuckin lunatic."

His voice is resentful. Studious. Concerned. Our friendship has been stretched, but not broken.

136

Wilbur yells out for us to get back to work.

The coffee break is over, but it still isn't light outside.

Suddenly, an hour after we eat, the work evaporates. Wilbur decides to go up to the grocery section to see if they need help, and Durango pretends anger: "Wilbur, you find anythin for us to do, I gonna stomp your ass!"

"Shut up, Durango," Wilbur says, climbing on a bug to make the trip up front.

"Christ," Durango says, holding his hands out in a semi-crucifixion, "you'd think we didn do *nothin* around here, the way you go an' volunteer our fuckin services!"

"Durango," Wilbur says, "the only thing bigger'n that nose of yours is your mouth."

Then he turns the ignition key of the bug and roars away.

"No shit," Durango says with a scholarly intonation, "that bastard is just askin for it."

Tubbs is climbing up onto a load of pallets, where he can sleep anytime. Durango and I go over and sit on a three-stack, which is just right. Durango lights a cigarette, exhales and says, "You know somethin, Soy Bean?"

"What?"

"I think I'm gonna dump that broad I been gone around with. You know, Sylvia Stevens."

"Why? What's the matter?"

Durango frowns. "Nothin' the matter, exactly, except she's gettin guilt feelings and all that shit. Christ, th'other day we just got through screwin, you know, and then you know what she starts talkin about?"

"What?"

"God, for Christ's sake. I mean, we just got through screwin, you know, and here we are lyin there in the goddam bed, balls-ass naked, and here she up and asks me do I believe in God, for Christ's sake!"

Durango is nervous, wary. He drags on his cigarette and exhales loudly. He doesn't even look at me, but runs a hand through his black hair.

"Christ, it makes me feel like crawlin outa my skin, for Christ's sake, her all the time askin about things like that and talkin about things like that."

"You say all the time?"

"Well, all the time lately."

For a few seconds we are silent, and then Durango—his profile still toward me—says, "You know somethin, Soy Bean? I been talkin a long time about this here Sylvia Stevens, but there's somethin, goddamit, I ain' told you."

"What's that?"

"Well, you see, she's got this here one thin leg. I mean, the other leg ain' *fat* or nothin . . . what I mean is, this here one leg is too thin, if you know what I mean. She had polio when she was a kid, or some goddam thing. She don' talk about it much. But one leg is definitely thinner than the other one."

There was nothing I could say to that, so I remained silent. And then I discovered something: Durango was sitting over there breathing fast and hard, like a man who's been running. I looked at him, but he still wasn't facing me. He was just sitting there breathing hard, his great shark-fin nose jutting out, and his lips compressed like a man who is about to blow a trumpet.

"Not that she ain' stacked. Man!" Now his voice is filled with awe. "God damn, she's got a pair of tits would make you drool at fifty feet. No shit. And a nice waist, and a little ass just meant to be grabbed."

I sit there drinking in Durango's words, half in love with Sylvia Stevens. Envious as hell. One little broomstick leg wouldn't make any difference to Ass-mad Asa M. Bean.

Durango shakes his fist in the air.

138

"I mean, all this guilt shit. You know what she asked me the last time? She asked me did I think we was doin wrong, havin intercourse. That's exactly the way she put it: 'havin intercourse'!"

"That's not entirely an unknown term for it," I say mildly.

"Shit, I know that, Soy Bean. Don't be so fuckin smart. I know that. But it was the way she asked it. I mean, shit, a man can pay too high a price for pussy!"

That last is going too far, I think, considering the state I am in, but I let the outrageous lie pass unchallenged.

Then Durango surprises me by asking if my father is alive.

"Half and half," I say. Then I explain that he is a permanent patient in a Methodist home for the elderly. Half-paralyzed and half-wacky.

"My father's dead," Durango says in a low voice. "You know what I wish?" When he asks this, he turns his face toward me.

"What?" I say.

"I only wish I could've gotten to know my father better. I was only nine when he died. But I bet he didn put up with no religious shit when it come to screwin."

"Probably not," I say.

"I mean, even if there is a God, Soy Bean, how's come we got peckers and snatches, if we wasn meant to use them?"

"A good question," I say. And mean it.

Durango laughs and says, "Man, I'll bet my old man was some cocksman before he died."

I have been avoiding Earlene ever since the demonstration. I know she's dying to talk to me about it. The girls in the demonstration made the late news that evening, and of course their pictures were in the newspapers.

In one of the pictures, I saw the guard with the rabbit's face. He looked a little irrelevant, and he also gave the impression of looking the wrong way, as if he wasn't sure exactly where the focus of activity was. (Anybody could have told him the focus of activity was the camera lens: I mean, who in the hell do you demonstrate *to?*)

But dinner is on the table and Earlene is calling up to me in my room, where I am sitting on the bed, brooding.

She calls several times before I dislodge myself, and march down the stairs and under the shining metal mobile and through the French doors into the dining room, where Earlene is helping little Debra eat her junior food. Earlene isn't looking at me, but she says, "Good heavens, Asa, I called four times. What were you doing up there?"

As I pull my chair out and sit down, I say, "I was sitting on the bed contemplating universals."

"He was contemplating his universal *joint,*" Roy corrects me, with his mouth full of hot German potato salad (one of his favorite foods). I condescend to look at him as he sits there in his underwear, jamming his big mouth with food and relieving himself of pronunciamentos. The sight of him discourages me. The minute the dumb ape gets in the house, he

140

takes off his clothes. I don't mind dumb apes, but I'm not sure I appreciate the fact that my sister has married one.

Debra makes cretinous noises, and I switch my gaze to her. She looks as if her mother has held her by her heels and dipped her head-first into a vat of stewed beets. She gives me a greasy red grin. Nobody expects anything from Uncle Asa but comedy. It occurs to me that my relationship to the world might be compulsively avuncular and comic. A terribly sad thought.

"I think women should concentrate on menstrating instead of de-menstrating," Roy says, carefully enunciating the pun.

I look at him, shocked that he would risk such a sarcasm (tearing of female flesh) at the dinner table. This second look, done to an obbligato of sizzling glances from Earlene, reveals that Roy is not only in his underwear (to be expected) but he's also drunk. The half glass of beer at his plate is flat. He's been downstairs guzzling while his brother-in-law was upstairs, communing with celestial verities.

Before I can gather myself together, Roy levels his loaded fork at Earlene, takes aim, and says, "Let me just ask you something, Earlene . . . right now while Asa's here to bear witness."

Debra stops chewing, and with her upper lip folded intensely over the lower, turns an anguished stare upward toward her father.

"Yes," Earlene says, "I'm waiting."

"Let me just ask this," Roy says, "do you consider yourself a woman first, or a wife first, or a mother first, or for Christ's sake a *sister* first?"

"I consider myself a *human being* first," Earlene says with dignity.

"Just as I suspected," Roy growls. One would have thought

that answer would put him in his place. But evidently it confirmed some dark inscrutable suspicion in his mind. He continues to shovel the food in, not lifting his eyes to anyone else. Debra starts gurgling, and Earlene suddenly grows large luminous tears in her eyes.

I think maybe I should jar them out of this sorry little impasse, so I ask Earlene how the demonstration went.

She darts a look at Roy and says, "See? Asa's every bit a man, and yet *he's interested!*"

Roy turns a slow look at me, and then says, "Yeah?" and returns to his food.

"What do you mean by that goddam 'yeah'?" I ask him. (God, what a meal! We're detonating all over the place.)

"Just what I said," Roy mumbles.

Asa casts a meditative look at the German potato salad. Earlene sniffs, but not from tears—from anger.

"Asa understands what we want," she says. "Don't you, Asa? You see, Roy, Asa isn't *threatened* by women the way *some* men are. He's secure and strong in his own masculine strengths and talents and . . . and security."

"Ace's not threatened by *anything,*" Roy says, reaching over and digging another pint of potato salad onto his plate. Then he eyes the ham, as if it's about to try to escape from him. "Ace's too far goddam out of it."

"*Asa understands women!*" Earlene shouts. Debra turns big eyes up to look at her mother who has just breathed fire on her innocent little shoulder.

"Yeah," Roy says, "well, let me ask you this: if Ace's so goddam understanding about women, how's come he suffers chronically from that Japanese disease?"

"What Japanese disease?" Earlene says, playing right into the playboy's hands.

"Lack-o'-nooky," Roy says triumphantly.

142

"Why don't you go somewhere and bleed to death?" I ask him.

"Roy!" Earlene cries. "Can't you ever think of little ears?"

"Through the eyes," I say.

"What?" Roy asks, turning a genuinely puzzled look toward me.

"Go somewhere and bleed to death through the eyes," I say. Then I say, "You look like you've gotten a good start already."

The conversation lags a little after that. Earlene sets Debra down from her chair, and my pretty little niece goes out into the front room, where the television has been growling all the time, like a caged beast under sedation.

"Well," Earlene says after a few minutes of silence, "if anyone just happens to be interested, I have an announcement to make: I'm pregnant. I went to the doctor today."

Then she starts crying and runs from the table. We hear her footsteps thumping on the stairway.

Silence.

Roy takes a few long breaths and stares biliously at the glass of flat beer in front of him.

"Son of a bitch," I say, sympathetically and respectfully.

Roy nods with a troubled look on his face.

"Thing is," he says after a few seconds, "she should have told *me* first. Alone. Just the two of us. I mean, this is no time to blurt it out, in an argument at the dinner table, for Christ's sake!"

"I see what you mean," I say.

"Ace," Roy says, "you know something? You're a pretty goddam nice guy, when all's said and done. I'm sorry if I insulted you a few minutes ago. It's just that this goddam FORCE thing is beginning to get me down. Shit, I don't know what the goddam women *want,* do you?"

143

I shake my head no, but more out of sympathy than agreement with the truth of what he's said.

Roy reads the clue, however. *"Do* you? Do you *honestly, really, truly* understand what in the shit all this furor is about? Because if you do, man, I mean, hell, I want to know too!"

"I suppose they want different things." The equivocation, at this point, seems necessary.

But the words apparently strike Roy with the impact of brilliance, and he sits there blinking a few minutes.

When he recovers, he says, "Well, sure, but hell, they're basically together. I mean, that's what a group is all about. And I've read their propaganda. I sympathize with a lot of it, like I've said a dozen times, but sometimes they go haywire. I mean, they contradict themselves: for example—and I told Earlene this just the other night—they want sexual freedom. Right? Okay. But they've still got to be women, which means the man gets on top. Okay? I don't mean all the time, but as the basic position."

I nod and look intelligent while Roy's voice gets scholarly. "And this is symbolic, if you know what I mean."

"Like the Apollonian solar deities and the chthonian female deities," I say, trying to rev things up a little bit.

Roy nods with the conviction of ignorance, and says, "Exactly."

But my interruption has broken the trajectory of his thought, and after a few seconds, he says, "I better go upstairs and calm Earlene down, and tell her how glad I am. Because I really am, you know. No shit. Really glad. I mean, it's not every day a man learns he's sired a second child. No sir! And it must be kind of tough on her getting pregnant when she's so involved in all this feminist work."

144

With that, Roy gets up from the table and makes his heavy-footed way through the kitchen and to the stairway. I hear him going up the stairs, and then Debra comes into the dining room, jabbering incoherently about something she's seen on television. Whatever it is, she wants her Uncle Asa to witness it. She takes one of my fingers in her fist, and leads me into the front room.

"And a little child shall lead them," I say.

Debra stops in front of the set.

"Debra," I ask her, "what's the secret of human existence, baby? Tell your Uncle Asa?"

She points at the set and says a word. I think the word is "whale," because that is what is shown rolling in the water, a big whale, with steam rising out of his spout.

I think of telling her the whale is really a floating water fountain, but I decide against it. The poor girl will have enough errors to swallow, digest and pass on, without her Uncle Asa adding to the poisonous heritage.

35

It is threatening snow again as I ride the bus back to Marlborough Heights. A heavy sack of cloud is washing biliously above us in the heavens, spitting a contemptuous flake upon the bare skin now and then, while the neon lights of the city have been turned on to luster like phosphorescent sea creatures in the hibernal gloom.

As I approach the house, I see Debra peering through the

window, looking for her Uncle Asa. Earlene's new drapes are pulled vastly to the side, so that this particular cherub may keep watch.

When I enter the house, she toddles up to me with her arms outstretched, so that I might pick her up. But before I lean over to gather her to my avuncular presence, I ask, "Debra, is there a God?"

She agitates her arms and utters something incoherent. I pick her up and jockey her to the television set.

Earlene enters the front room, wearing slacks. Her hair is in curlers, making her eyes look a little slanted.

"So it's you," she says.

"It was the last time I looked," I say. "How do you feel?"

"Oh, I'm fine," she says. But her manner isn't fine; her manner is quasi-grim. Mini-grim.

"I meant about your being *enceinte*," I say with aloof fraternal delicacy.

"I know exactly what you meant," she says.

"All right," I say. "What's up?"

"You know," she says, "I could have died when I saw you there at the art museum. What were you doing to that picture?"

My face starts to burn and I mumble something into my beard.

"What?" she says, raising her voice.

"I said I was about to slash it with my sword."

"Oh Asa, you wouldn't!" Earlene cries. "That's exactly what I thought."

"Well anyway, I didn't."

"I could have died when I saw you standing there," she said.

I glance at her face to see if there is concealment or irony there; but there isn't. I slip out to the kitchen for a beer. Obvi-

146

ously, Earlene hadn't detected the shameful state I was in.

Or *was* I in a shameful state? The intensity and confusion of the moment, the distracted sensibility of ass-mad, bashful old Asa . . . his frenetic imagination boiling ideas and images in a constant bubbling stew of passions and alarms. . . .

Then it occurs to me: why should the future always be held in thrall to the past? Why cannot a man create himself anew? Create the past, as surely as the future! What about the existential leap, Don Roderigo?

(Who's Don Roderigo?)

What about the ichthyic leap, then?

Asa Bean, Reborn.

St. Asa in his study.

St. Asa, Redivivus et Recidivus.

All is one and the same.

All is hazy at the edges.

Heraclitus steps into a river, slips on the backs of a myriad silver chubs and goes floating downstream, shouting axioms in a terrified voice.

Hazy Bean drinks from the can of Miller's High Life and decides (all hail) that he did not expose himself in front of the canvas.

But even if he did, the picture was that of a plump *female* nude. Nothing wrong with old Asa: if he is to be demented, he will certainly not stoop to perversion.

No one saw what I may or may not have done.

I will therefore be free to walk the streets and perpetuate further outrages in the arena of my mind (sic).

Earlene is talking to me, exactly four feet beyond the periphery of my attention. She is talking about poor Father.

Debra is tugging at the knee of my pant leg.

I lean over and say to her, "Our birth is but a sleep and a forgetting."

Earlene interrupts her monologue and says, "Asa, are you listening to me?"

I turn to her, point my index finger upward and say, "The Soul that rises with us, our life's Star, hath had elsewhere its setting, and cometh from afar."

Earlene casts her eyes at the ceiling and says, "What on earth are you *talking* about?"

Debra says something, and I turn back and face the sweet and warm little star of her face, drifting upon the silken waters of the moment: "Not in entire forgetfulness," I continue, "and not in utter nakedness, but trailing clouds of glory do we come, from God, who is our home."

"Asa!" Earlene shouts, "will you kindly stick to the subject? And will you kindly stop tormenting that poor confused little thing?"

"Debra understands every word I say."

"She does not," Earlene says.

"She does too."

"She does not."

"Does *too!*"

"Asa, stop it this instant!"

Earlene's voice is so loud and anguished that Debra starts to cry. She was really calm until my sister had to open her big mouth.

36

This afternoon, after work, I rewrote parts of my article on Deianira's robe, and muddled around my room, trying to make up my mind about calling Madge Hunter.

It was beginning to seem a little arbitrary, somehow. I did my best to remember whether Madge had really manifested any interest in my idea. And for the life of me, I couldn't even remember how much I had discussed it with her.

But in the forum of my mind, the Counter-Sophist arose and made it quite clear that the material I was concerned with in the article *must* be of interest to an intelligent woman in the feminist movement.

Suddenly, I hear Roy downstairs. His presence is announced by the soft plunk of the refrigerator door closing. I can almost see him standing in his stocking feet, as he pops the cap off a Miller's High Life.

Maybe a beer will help.

I go downstairs, and Earlene intercepts me in the hallway.

"I've just been talking on the phone to Madge Hunter," she says, something insidiously triumphant in her eyes.

"I just came down for a beer," I tell her.

"Help yourself," Roy says, which is extraordinarily generous of him, considering I have bought the beer.

When I take my first long cold drink, Earlene comes up to me and pats me on my shoulder. It is almost a masculine gesture, and so much unlike Earlene that I am jumpy.

"I think Madge has discovered the secret," she says.

When I don't say anything, Roy calls out from the living room, "What secret?"

"The secret of what makes Asa tick."

"Hell, that's no secret," Roy says. "Lack-o'-nooky."

"No, it's not that. That's only part of it."

An important part; and getting more important every day, every hour. I almost say this, but wisely remain quiet.

"Defenses," Earlene whispers to me. "Fear and intelligence. Fear of showing how much you need women, and intelligence to conceal this need."

149

"Big deal," I say, trying to sound as contemptuous as the occasion demands. "Big Ass Deal."

"Will you two talk louder so I can hear?" Roy says, coming into the kitchen.

Earlene turns toward him, and says, "Madge has really found the key to the mysterious antics of my brother," she says.

"So you just said," Roy mumbles. "Is that all?"

We gab pointlessly for a few minutes, and then Earlene tells me that we have received another letter from Father. She fetches it for me, and I sit down, prepared to be depressed for a few minutes. The letter reads:

Dear Children,

I am still alive, and my mood is as good as can be expected. Take comfort and do not be distressed when I die. Do not be beguiled by the people around you; in every historical period, the world has been largely comprised of fools, and why should it be different now? Remember the commandment to love, even if you forget all else. Remember the verse, "Better is a dinner of herbs where love is, than a stalled ox and hatred therewith." (Proverbs 15, I think; but then my memory is uncertain these days.)

Is your mother dead? I can't remember. Where is she?

Love,
Dad

Earlene breaks into tears when I finished the letter, even though I had read it silently.

"I can't stand those letters," she says.

"He seems pretty lucid in this one," I say. "Except for that last thing, about Mother."

"Do you really think so?"

I'm not sure, now that she asks. I am thinking of love, and suddenly I am aware that Madge Hunter is a dinner of herbs,

150

if there ever was one, and who wants a stalled ox anyway?

In a fury of determination, I go to the phone and tell her I am bringing over the Deianira article.

Praise be, she consents. She even tells me she is going to be home all evening, and has nothing planned. Nothing whatsoever.

I am in a fog of longing, of desire; I am caught up in an argument of lascivious intent.

Madge Hunter, wait for me!

I will ardently carry your banners, lusty bitch!

Avail.

37

The bus is fairly crowded for this time of evening, and I half regret not walking to Madge Hunter's apartment. For one thing, I have to take this bus most of the way downtown, and then transfer to another that will deposit me within three blocks of her place.

While I am riding, I think briefly of Veronica, and then let her image slip away from me. She is too pathetic to think of, suddenly. And too confusing. (Has Durango come between us?) Not only that, the lecher inside me keeps tilting Madge Hunter's image into extraordinarily erotic postures. Poor Madge's blood would go to her poor head if she only knew what was happening to her hapless simulacrum.

Watch out, Madge! Asa M. Bean is journeying toward you, tumid with lustful juices and frenetic from the clash of ironic armies within his breast!

My progress is dreamlike. Success upon success. Successfully I get off at the correct place, and successfully board the correct bus that will convey my awesome burden of desire within three blocks of her address.

Uncanny. Asa Bean gets off the bus at the correct street, and successfully walks along the icy sidewalks toward the apartment of the local coordinator of FORCE. He trembles with anticipation, unused to such compounded efficacy.

The neighborhood is middle-class. Brick doubles and duplexes, with arborvitae lining the drives, and red berry shrubs snuggled against the houses.

Madge's address is that of a small, pink, brick apartment house, with reticulated lead windows giving a phony Tudor quality to the structure.

I walk up the cement walk that curves like a question mark to the front door. I step inside, and look at the four mail slots on the right wall. Above each mail slot is a small white card, with a name on it. The last has "M. Hunter" in pale gray script. Behind the name is the number 4.

The only two doors visible on the first floor are numbered 1 and 2; and with rare perspicacity, I deduce that numbers 3 and 4 are upstairs.

I climb the steps with my heart thudding. The manuscript on Deianira is rolled tightly in my right hand, both thrust into my pocket. The manuscript is now a little damp with sweat.

When I reach the number 4, I pause briefly, and knock. There is silence to the count of three, and then the door swings open.

Madge smiles and invites me in. The smile seems a little less confident than it was the other night, however. But can this be so?

Madge is wearing a short dark skirt, reaching only halfway down her splendid, clean-looking thighs, and a soft peach blouse. I shoot a brief glance at the blouse to see if she's wearing a bra, but the look tells me nothing, and I turn away in confusion, tasting blood in my mouth.

"Well," she says, adjusting her glasses, "how about a drink? I have Scotch, is that all right? Scotch and soda?"

"Fine," I say.

She turns her back and goes into the kitchen. The apartment is a little like Veronica's—about the same size and vintage. But it doesn't have the air of madness that permeates Veronica's apartment, and suddenly I am happy to be here. Not just excited, but happy.

Careful, Asa; don't panic.

Keep thy mouth shut!

We owe it to others to be happy, I think. And whatever her shortcomings (being a trifle mad, for example), Madge Hunter is happy. Or seems happy.

Maybe she doesn't know any better. I can understand that.

She returns to the sofa, where I am sitting, and hands me my Scotch and soda.

I drink deeply of the Pictian potion, exhale, smack my lips. I am fabricating sounds of ease, of contentment, of leisure. My stomach is as tense as the rear coil spring of an overloaded truck.

Madge is also acting cool. Or (is it possible?) she *is* cool.

I grope for something to say. I take another sip, smack my lips again, and then remember good old dependable Deianira.

"The thing that really fascinates me is the robe," I say.

Madge Hunter turns her head slowly (cyanotropic) to look at me. Our eyes lock in deadly recognition. There is a tiny smile tugging cozily at the corners of her lips.

She shakes her head wonderingly. "Talk on," she says. "Talk on!" (What is there about Asa Bean that causes people to repeat themselves?)

153

"Deianira's robe. I have the first draft. It's my idea that this is a female symbol. It's woven, created by women's hands. It's warm and enclosing. And an entrapment. You know what Deianira means in Greek?"

Madge shakes her smiling head no. "I've no idea," she says.

" 'Render or tearer of a man, or husband!' "

"Wow!" Madge says.

"You see, I'm one person who still takes Bachofen seriously."

Madge frowns and adjusts her glasses. "Who's that?"

"Bachofen?"

"Yes."

For an instant, my mind is blank. Who am *I*? I ask myself. What am I doing here? Why am I not sailing the seas of my mysterious, thalassic Madge, my Wise Woman, my Diotima, my Hecate, my warm pussy. Yes, let it be said: my Deianira.

Who *am* I? What populations constitute my heritage at this juncture of apocalypse?

Oh Asa, you stand in danger of losing yourselves.

"Who's that?" Madge asks again, patiently, drawing a circle on my wrist with her index finger.

The act fills me with electricity. I am a giant transformer, a generator of lust, a Monster of desire.

"Who's *that?*" she asks again, and I mumble something about Bachofen's theory of *Mutterecht,* his seeing the history of Greece in terms of an unacknowledged, even unconscious strife between ascendant male and thwarted female values.

"The robe, the robe," I say, shaking my head with the wonder of it.

"Ridiculous," Madge Hunter says, taking my empty glass, the ice cubes chattering amongst themselves, from my hand and walking calmly into the kitchen.

"The-Robe-as-Net," I articulate distinctly in the direction of the opposite wall.

She is standing in front of me, holding forth another drink. "Here," she says. "The mouth is made for more than talking. Or haven't you read that yet?"

Her sarcasm stings me. I answer, "Yes, for drinking."

"Oh for that, too, I suppose," Madge Hunter says. Agreeable, indulgent, kissable Madge.

"You really need someone to take care of you, don't you?" she says. She is sitting next to me, her warm thigh pressed cozily against mine. No longer is she tracing inscrutable configurations on my bare wrist, but she is gazing at me seriously, with interest and—is it possible?—understanding.

Not only that, it occurs to me that she might even be *friendly* toward me. Can this be true?

"Oh, you do play fantastic tricks, don't you, Asa?"

"I do, I do."

"*Why* do you play fantastic tricks?"

"Various reasons," I say.

"Oh, come on!"

"It's true."

"Wouldn't it be nice," she says, "if we didn't have to perform, didn't have to be intelligent? Wouldn't it? Honestly? For just a *little, teensy, weensy* while, anyway?"

She clutches my wrist and squeezes. "Answer me," she says.

"Maybe."

"Is that all, Asa? *Maybe?*"

"Maybe."

Madge laughs and takes a drink, and I hear a random ice cube clack obstreperously against her white teeth.

"Oh, Asa!" she says, after a silence that seems to be two hours and twenty minutes long.

"I just thought you would be interested in the article," I explain.

"I am," she says. "Honestly, I'd just *love* to read it. But some other time, Asa. All right? Now we can relax and enjoy our drink and things like that."

"The irony is exquisite: as in all Greek tragedy, Deianira gets exactly what she's been asking for. I mean, she captures Hercules, but in the act destroys them. I mean, him. A typical female ambivalence, if you see what I mean. What women want, Madge, is a man they can't quite throw the old robe around. The eternal dialectic, erotic dance. You know, the Greek chorus is a physical paradigm of dialectic. Or Chinese: Yin and yang."

I must be half-drunk. Seldom do I botch things quite like this. I finish my drink, and Madge says, "Let me suggest something. Okay?"

"What?"

She looks thoughtfully at my right ear, a nibbly little twitch working at her lips.

"Starting right now, for each drink we take, we take off exactly one article of clothing. No more, no less."

God! She has cast the robe!

My head roars like a brace of speedboats, and I laugh nervously. "You could make an alcoholic out of me that way!" I say.

"Never mind," she says, smiling. "You don't have to say clever things. Just play the game with me. That is, if you're interested."

"I'm interested," I say, my voice so hoarse it is scarcely audible. I start to tell her that I've never said a less clever thing in my whole life, but wisely I remain silent.

We both take a sip, and Madge takes off one shoe. I remove my tie. I think we smile at each other; at least, Madge

156

smiles at me, and then she says, "You can talk if you want to, Asa. But promise you won't just talk to be clever."

"I promise." I swallow, and take another drink; but Madge hasn't taken another.

Then she says something that spirals a muted surprise through me, although the passion of the moment will not let me dwell upon it. "Listen," she says, stroking my wrist. "I'm going to take all the irony out of you this evening. Nobody can even get near you, Asa, the way you talk. And, so help me, I'm going to cure you of that. At least temporarily."

I sit for a minute looking at her sweet knees and trying to understand her words.

"Go on," she says. "You've got to take off something else."

"But you didn't drink," I say.

"There's no requirement to drink together," she says. (Female perfidy!) Then she leans over and unties my left shoe. Dumbly, I wait until she finishes and grabs the shoe with both hands; and then I put my right foot against the back of the left, and help her slide the shoe off.

She laughs. I'm a marionette, and she holds all my trembling nerves like strings in her hands. "Come on," she says. "Don't look so lugubrious. Here. I'll drink again. I'm not going to trick you."

She takes a sip, and then flips her other shoe halfway across the room.

"See?" she says.

"I do."

Then, nervously I take another drink, and kick off my other shoe simultaneously. When I lower the glass, she is smiling at me over hers.

She takes off one stocking, and I take off my shirt.

"Ooooh," she says. "You've got muscles. Look at those shoulders!"

"It's the work I do," I mumble, pleased underneath all the fifes and drums of my lust. "Always hustling heavy crates of lettuce around. And things."

"I'll bet," she says.

Then she takes a long drink, and leans over to pull her other stocking off. "Come on," she says. "Be fair. Especially since men wear more things than women do."

I take a drink and pull off both socks.

"That's nice," she says, apparently forgetting the rules. "You doubled up."

"I suppose you think that's symbolic," I say.

"Which?" she asks.

"Women wearing fewer clothes than men."

"Well, isn't it?"

"I don't know," I say. Then I can't stand it any longer, and I reach over and put my arm around her and kiss her on the mouth. Her lips open for me, and my hand eases over her heart breast, which is warm and soft and unencumbered by a bra.

"Now you know my secret," she says. "So just stay back. You're not supposed to touch. Not yet, anyway. Just drink and undress."

"What do you call this game, anyway?" Asa Bean, the Compulsive Verbalist, asks her.

"Oh, just about anything you want. I like to think of it as 'Bedroom Billiards.' "

I don't get the "billiards" part, but I'm not interested in asking.

When we take our next drink, I remove my trousers, and Madge removes her skirt. She is wearing panties, with her peach blouse hanging outside. Her eyes are wet-looking behind her glasses.

158

She pats me quickly and says, "Now *that* is what I would call 'being in a manly state.'"

By now, we are both half-mad with lust and I say, "Why don't you take off your glasses."

"No," she says. "I want to see."

We drink again, and I take off my undershirt, and Madge takes off her blouse. Her breasts are small and lovely, and the nipples, as fifty paperback novels in every drugstore and bus station in the country would tell us, are hard with passion.

I caress them, and kiss her mouth, and then with a burst of impatience, scoop her out of her panties, throw my own shorts on the floor, and push her back on the sofa. She is warm and moist for me, and within a few seconds, she is digging her fingernails into my back and moaning as we thrash our way home.

For the rest of the evening we talk and screw and talk and screw some more.

She is a marvelous woman, with an uncommonly low threshold of passion.

I spend the night there, and when the alarm clock rings at 4:00 A.M., Madge Hunter rises from her bed, sleepy and happy and befuddled, and cooks breakfast for me.

When I leave, we kiss each other, and have one last feel. Then she says, "You were beautiful, Asa. You made me come every time."

I kiss her again, and thank her for all her gifts.

There is no irony left in me, and no intelligence.

I am now Roy.

I am now Durango.

I go to the bus line, warm inside, while the cold winds whirr past me, flipping my coat back and burning my eyes and cheeks.

Boarding the bus, I realize that I have forgotten to deliver the manuscript to Madge. It is still there inside my pocket, full of my thoughts about Deianira's robe.

Asa Bean knows what that robe is. He can name it and explain its alchemic properties.

The morning is dark and frigid outside.

The bus (female) carries its passengers into the night, searching out its way with the two-pronged yellow lights extending like a great vaporous tuning fork into the darkness. Journeying forward into the future, she carries little Asa Bean, like a newborn possum, into his own most essential fate.

Peace.

I am happy. I am content.

All praise to Madge Hunter.

Ave.

Avail.

The Assassin is already dead; the Shawnee is languishing in a non-referential limbo.

38

Rosy-Digited Dawn dabs the dusty windows of the warehouse pink. We have finished unloading a potato car, and I stand at the boxcar's opening, atop the ramp that Tubbs and Durango drive their bugs up to where Wilbur and I have to load the hundred-pound sacks on pallets.

A geometrically perfect shadow extends along one window, angling in and out of the well with a precision that could take your breath away, if you had the nerve to take it all in and contemplate its miraculousness.

Wilbur is in a foul mood, and taciturn. Tubbs has hurt his back, and is good for little else but bug duty.

Inside the warehouse, we hear them roaring down the aisles, fading in and out as they approach or depart. It is Durango's turn to pick up this pallet load, and I contemplate him in my imagination as he slices the darkness with his shark nose, beady eyes searching out the hole wherein he must place the load.

Durango, also, is taciturn, leaving only Tubbs and myself in good spirits—Tubbs with his wrenched back and Asa Bean, with his altered fate.

Several times I think of batty, old, sweet old Madge Hunter, and so help me, my loins and genitals turn warm. Her glow fills my viscera, lungs, heart and brain. It warms my hands and knees.

Madge, my sweet hot burner, keeps me warm. Perhaps, I think, she also feels the sun break out upon her flesh at odd moments, while she's working . . . feels me radiate through all her cells with sudden hot showers of remembered sperm.

Durango returns, and still refuses to look at me. When I ask him a question, he answers in monosyllables. He has actually refrained from foul language in my presence, which with Durango symbolizes enormous withdrawal and rejection. He talks to me as if he were speaking over the telephone.

The day passes elusively, nothing really happening. Several times I brood upon that apocalyptic scene in the art museum, wondering what the apocalypse really was.

As I work, I also clothe myself in silence. It is comfortable. Wilbur takes the hint, too, and reduces his gab to whistling a medley of unrecognizable tunes.

In the art museum. I remember it clearly. I remember all those women lined up, singing that asinine song about Rubens and harlotry. I remember their sassy voices, and wonder if they were experiencing anything remotely like self-irony.

No, self-irony is a male obsession, a male preoccupation, a male invention. The nearest women can achieve to it, bless their ovaries, is a certain sassiness. That's what they were: sassy. They were sassing the world made by men (allegedly), and having a marvelous time doing it.

Sassy Earlene and sassy Madge standing there in the Rubens display room, while ass-mad Asa leans forward into the image of a painted woman, and contemplates all the delicious fruits of her rape.

This was the first step! I see it now.

For this is when Madge first understood the imprisonment of my self-directed irony. What ironic man can make love? And yet, how can man achieve truth, humanity, understanding, humor, manhood, without irony?

Oh Madge, we were made for each other!

You were victorious: when you said you would divest me of all irony, my sweet musky mink, my hot bristling bitch, you did. You did. You did.

But listen, my vixen, my sweet knees: when I put on my clothes, I once more invested myself with the old irony, and once more escaped your impossible sanity.

Which (my liberation) of course you need as much as I. What good is conquest without escape? Man and woman: the dialectic dance, always to be tried anew, tried again, in the constant ceremony of discovery. *Vive,* l'endeavored dance! Always tried, always achieved.

Near one o'clock, we learn that the grocery section needs help, so we have the opportunity of two hours overtime. Durango and Tubbs refuse, but Wilbur and I take the chance. I have decided to buy Madge something nice. An extra seven dollars will help me in my impulse.

Actually, the overtime extends still an extra hour, so when I ring out, I am very tired. But maybe a quick beer at The Fifth Wheel will help out, so Wilbur—who doesn't drink— gives me a ride.

He pulls up into the parking lot, and we are sitting there with the engine idling for a couple of minutes, gossiping about the grocery section. It is a comfortable moment, filled with lazy conversation before I get out of the car and Wilbur drives on. Neither of us is hurried.

Then we see fat old Todhunter, wearing a short-sleeved white shirt in the cold, carry out a big aluminum can of garbage to the incinerator in back. He is carrying it in one hand, the other beefy arm flailing in rhythm with each step to help him keep balance.

Wilbur and I are silent an instant, and then Wilbur says, "There's Durango."

I look up, and indeed it is Durango, escorting Veronica to his Mustang, which I haven't even noticed parked right there in front of us, about six cars away.

It is uncertain whether or not Durango has seen us. He looks preoccupied, morose. But this is how he's been lately.

I haven't told him about Madge yet. His betrayal of me, and the consequent remoteness of his manner, coincided exactly with the conquest of Madge the Huntress over my eagerly accepting flesh.

"Looks like he's beating your time," Wilbur says in his flat voice.

I am about to express a factitious bitterness: that this is merely another example of the triumph of the crude and vulgar over the subtle and refined . . . that the world itself, not men, drove *all* of us to harlotry; that we are corrupted by the air we breathe, for always the crass seem to triumph over the excellent. What greater cause is there for neurosis than this? Man's witness of the perverse inequity of the structure about him is more of a cause for neurosis than the Freudian's Oedipal dreams or the existentialist's canonization of the Fear of Death.

I am about to speak these things, when I am stopped by a truly surprising thought: in the context of my present contentment, I don't really *mind* Durango's betrayal and conquest. If Madge hadn't seduced me (*unimaginable* contingency) it would be another matter; but as it is, Madge can give me all I want.

So there it is: I was betrayed . . . cuckolded, almost. And I have justifiable grounds for resentment. The fact that the grounds are justifiable is perhaps the greatest temptation of all for a human being, especially when the grounds are merely justifiable, and not real.

Who is not tempted by the insidious appeal of a superficial wrong?

At this silent and humble moment, Asa M. Bean—beyond the purview of Wilbur's care and understanding—learns something good and honorable.

And he forgives Durango for a wrong that was only appearance, and therefore no wrong at all.

Surely, this is heroic: to forgive those who only seem to have wronged us. Those who have really wronged us are, indeed, the easiest to forgive.

A humble miracle has passed through the thoughts of Asa Bean, and he gets out of the door, thanking Wilbur for the ride. He goes inside The Fifth Wheel, orders a beer, drinks it down, and then goes to catch his bus.

Things are quiet at home. In fact, no one is there. Earlene has taken Debra shopping with her and hasn't returned yet, although it is almost six o'clock. Roy is working late.

I go upstairs and lie down on my bed. I think of Madge, and wish that she were available tonight, but she has told me that she has a meeting with FORCE. Tomorrow, we'll have dinner together at her apartment. She doesn't like to go to restaurants, which fact puts her in the top 3 percentile of American womanhood, according to the A. Bean scale.

As I drift off to sleep, I listen for the bushes to rustle. But nothing happens, no one comes. I let the old-fashioned newsreel start unwinding, but the dark streets are empty. I gaze for several minutes at the Assassin's window, but steadfastly it, too, remains empty.

They will not appear as long as I wear my Badge. They have been exorcised by the cunning of the local coördinator of FORCE, who, with the same deft pelvic strokes and loving gestures by the body's cries (older than newts, terrapins, reptilian birds and all classes of cephalopods), rendered all masterpieces suddenly safe and perdurable.

Madge, you have helped me find myself hiding there among myselves. For when there is irony, there is more than oneself, and by extirpating irony, you have consolidated me into a single name, Asa Mark Bean.

At least when the lens of what you are is focusing me. (Hark, that was another voice speaking! Can it be? It can. Thus perpetuatcth itself the dance.)

But for this once and this oneness, Madge, and speaking for myselves, we love you.

Sweet bifurcated magician who unifies my songs into one harmony, all hail.

Your throbbing is from the engines of grace and perfec-

tion. Each of your cells is a star. We celebrate you, I do.
I love you, Madge, we do.

All hail.

39

"Hey, Soy Bean, I got somethin to talk over'th you."

"Shoot."

"Naw, shit, man! This ain' no place to do it. Here, lemme refill your coffee cup. I'll do you a favor. Okay?"

"Isn't it time to get back to work?"

"Naw, Wilbur's up in the front office, sniffin that broad's chair. So come on, you can drink another cup of coffee. How about it, man?"

"Okay."

"I just wanted to talk to you a couple minutes now to see if I could talk to you later. You know what I mean?"

"Sure."

"Hell, this ain' no place to talk. How you gone say anything serious with all these morons around? This here's somethin serious I got to talk over'th you."

"How about the Fill'th you, sometimes known as The Fifth Wheel?"

"Sure, that's what I said. Didn't I say The Fifth Wheel?"

"No, you didn't say anywhere."

"Didn I just now say The Fifth Wheel, before I offered to refill your fuckin coffee cup?"

"Not that I heard. All I heard was you wanted to talk to me later. I didn't hear you say anything about The Fifth Wheel."

"You *sure,* man?"

"Certain. Sure. Positive."

"Christ, I would've sworn I said The Fifth Wheel. I must be slippin my fuckin *gears,* the way things been gone lately."

"Things fall apart."

"You ain' just shittin, man! Here. Here's your coffee."

"Thanks."

"Tell you what, Soy Bean: I'll buy you a beer when we get to The Fifth Wheel."

"Good. Sounds great."

"Cause I really wan' talk to you, know what I mean?"

"Sure. It's a nice place. We can talk there."

"Exactly. Exactly what I figured. We can drink a beer and talk."

"Sure, you can lay it on me, right?"

"Exactly what I had in mind, man!"

"Here comes Wilbur. Coffee break's over."

"Shit."

40

After work, we proceed to The Fifth Wheel, accompanied by an obbligato of engine clanking from Durango's Mustang. Durango is pale, serious, intent. A frown cleaves his forehead where the shark-fin nose leaves off. His beard darkens. His lips are sucked in.

When I get out of the car, I brush my red ski cap against the roof and knock it off into the slush.

"Absit omen," I say, and Durango says, "What?"

"I was merely speaking the language of your fathers," I say.

"Hey, you speak Wop?" Durango asks.

"No, Latin."

"Jesus Christ," Durango says.

"No, he spoke Aramaic."

But Durango is troubled, and does not respond to wit. He slouches ahead of me with his hands in his pockets. He always walks this way, as if he's never warm, never quite at ease.

Inside The Fifth Wheel, Veronica comes up to our booth and gets our order. She doesn't look at either one of us.

When she leaves, neither of us watches the wandering, glorious, moving, planetary circus of her ass, because we both know. Durango is troubled, uneasy, jumpy, depressed.

So I decide to tell him. "I've got a girl friend, Durango."

"You what?"

"A girl friend. I screwed her eighty-three times the other night."

"Come on!" Durango cries. "What you talking about, man?"

"My problems are solved. She's simpatico. Speaks intellectual shit, as you once put it so memorably."

"Not Veronica there," Durango says, relief brightening his face.

"No, this is a broad you don't know, Durango."

His face relaxes and he takes a long drink. "Son of a bitch," he says, exhaling beer fumes in a miasma of relief.

"She's really fabulous . . . a real piece of tail," I say, translating for him.

"Son of a bitch," Durango says. "Old Soy Bean the Cocksman!"

"That is an epithet," I say slowly, "that has not often come to mind within the past year or so."

168

"Son of a bitch," Durango says.

When Veronica takes our next order, I pay. She smiles tentatively at both of us, cued by some mysterious signal from Durango.

"Son of a bitch," Durango says, after she leaves the booth.

I stare at him for an instant. He catches my eyes briefly, looks uncomfortable, and then lifts his beer and sips loudly.

"Durango," I say slowly, and with great emphasis, "I forgive you."

"You *what,* man?"

"I forgive you."

"Soy Bean, what the fuck you talkin about now?"

"It's as simple as the nose on your face, the beer in your glass, the Budweiser in your veins," I say. "I forgive you."

Durango's eyebrows climb toward the ceiling. He lifts two identical imponderables with both hands, palm upward. "You forgive me *what,* Soy Bean?"

"Anything you want. Take your pick. I forgive you."

"Soy Bean, sometimes I'm worried about you. No shit."

"Lust and be happy," I say.

"Never in my whole fuckin life I know anybody talks the way *you* talk, Soy Bean. No shit. Never!"

"Be thou happy. Take no thought for your sins. You are forgiven. I forgive you."

"Shit," Durango says, eyebrows raised once more, pouring himself more beer, "if you want to play *that* game, Soy Bean, I'll tell you what: I'll forgive *you,* too."

We touch glasses in a toast. Veronica is out of sight momentarily.

"What you think of that?" Durango says.

"I consider that simply splendid," I say.

"Son of a bitch," Durango says, shaking his head back and forth with the enormity of his bewilderment.

169

"Succinctly put," I say. "And with a certain memorable suggestion of the ambiguous. *Curiosa felicitas,* as your ancestors put it so well."

"Hey, come off it, will you? My folks come from Sicily, for Christ's sake."

"Son of a bitch," I say, and we both drink.

41

Madge has had me for dinner. She is no Pythagorean in her approach to the erotic arts with Asa, her beloved Bean. Like the praying mantis, she chewed my numbly ecstatic head off while we were copulating.

But like the dialectic, Heraclitean earthworm, I grew another while she wasn't looking.

Ah, we will go on like this forever.

We are to be married. *Mirabile dictu.*

For she is a warm magician, a priestess of love. She is a wondrously skillful cook, a dopey, mixed-up warm-hearted, shrewd, pragmatic, passionate woman, incapable of really taking men or ideas seriously for long, a natural organizer, a wobbly thinker, a devoted Forcean, full of misinformation and deadly insights. (She maintains that I have exsights; but this is the index of her humor, and I will thrive in her presence.)

I see myself a score of years from now, fat, venerable, and wise, surrounded by little Debra-like creatures, my numberless progeny seeking erudition at my knees. Philoprogenitive Ace-eye. I will pause, withdraw my pipe from my mouth, and speak to them in Latin.

Late in the evening, when the fire is low and I have tired of editing the manuscript for my fortieth book on various recondite subjects, Madge will attack me from the darkened kitchen, and we will lust upon the rug, the sofa, the Boston rocker, while the *kinder* snooze above our heads and dream of sugar bunnies.

I shall burn out suddenly and gratuitously at the age of ninety-three, and then turn holy.

All these fantasies wheel in my head as I soak in the tub, warm water laving my tired muscles. It has been a hard day, and somewhere in the far reaches of the house, little Debra is practicing her echolalia.

The door slams, and I hear Roy shout, "I sold it! I sold it!"

All joy to the Scobie house, for surely he is referring to the apartment house. As I loll in the tub, I smile with pleasure that my own brother-in-law seems to be succeeding. His joy will radiate upon Earlene, little Debra, and the yet-unknown creature now ensconced beneath Earlene's lungs and liver.

As Roy Scobie himself observed: "A family is like a finely tuned mechanism."

Asa, it is time for thy departure. Hasten thy marriage and depart.

As I open the drain and stand up in the tub, I say aloud: "I will, I will."

"Did you say something?" Earlene calls from the other side of the bathroom door.

"No, just talking to myself," I say.

"Did you hear?" Earlene cries joyfully. "I came up to tell you! Roy sold the apartment house! We're rich! We're rich!"

"Wonderful, wonderful!" I cry.

Truth to tell, I am pleased for various reasons. I have found that when Marxists are poor, they are invariably ill-tempered, and of course this sale will give a boost to Roy's morale.

"Isn't that marvelous?" Earlene cries, walking away from the door.

"Marvelous, marvelous," I repeat, stepping out of the tub.

When I go downstairs, we all have a jolly beer over Roy's good luck. It is Roy's second beer.

We toast one another; in fantasy, we spend Roy's money in fantastic ways—tours to Latin America, a swimming pool in back, a new Cadillac with spotlights at the side.

"That reminds me, Asa," Earlene says, "that man called again."

"What reminds you?" I ask.

"Does it make any *difference?*" Earlene asks. "Don't you even want to know who it *was?*"

"I know who it was," I say. "I want to know what reminded you."

"All right then, smarty, who was it?"

"Jim Talbot."

Earlene drops her jaw and turns a cretinously wondering stare toward Roy. "How on earth did he guess *that?*" she asks him.

"Don't ask me," Roy says calmly. "He's your brother."

"How did you know?" Earlene asks me.

"Well," I say, "Madge is working, and not only that, she isn't a man; secondly, no one else would call me. Except maybe Durango."

Suddenly I am aware that I have somehow dampened things by guessing who it was. Earlene wanted to inform me of something, and I was rude enough, boorish enough, to anticipate her.

Oh, Asa, will you ever learn?

With luck, no.

Roy is undisturbed, however; he is still euphoric over the sale. He has taken off his pants, but his shirt (crescents of perspiration stain at the armpits) is still on, and his tie is twisted to the side. The hairs of his balding head are mussed and his eyes are distant.

Debra toddles through the kitchen, bumps into her mother's leg, and falls down.

I go, "Boom," and she gets up, laughing heartily.

It is time to tell them. It is time to jettison this happy family, and let them live their own lives. Especially since there is another little Scobie, even now, even at this instant, making up his mind, hand, and body to join the world.

"We are to be married, Madge and I."

There. I have said it.

The silence is centripetal, flying back into my face, where it rests like a fuzzy, somewhat awkward bird.

"You *what?*" Earlene asks.

"Madge Hunter and I have decided to become one."

"One *what?*" Roy asks, and then brays a three-second laugh at the ceiling.

"One flesh, one spirit," I say in a voice that sounds a little offended.

"Son of a bitch," Roy says, spiraling down into something approximating understanding. At least, belief.

"Asa," Earlene cries, "you're not serious!"

"Serious is precisely what I am. Serious. Determined. Decided. And, as a matter of fact, awfully pleased at the prospect."

"Son of a bitch," Roy says, trying it with a slightly different tone.

"Look at it this way," I say, "you're not losing a brother-in-law so much as you're gaining a sister-in-law. Although I guess there's thin comfort in that."

"Oh, Asa," Earlene cries, "I'm so happy!"

She would be.

And as females sometimes do in real life as well as in movies, my sister demonstrates her joy by breaking into great spasms of weeping.

"Therefore, of course," I say, when the gusts have subsided somewhat, "I shall be leaving this good place for another."

"Of course," Roy says, still smiling. Undoubtedly he smiles with the realization that now, after the apartment building sale, he will be able to afford whole breweries for his thirst, instead of mere cases of Miller's High Life.

"Oh, Asa, I'm so happy," Earlene says.

Even little Debra seems awed by the occasion, and sits upon the floor—a tattered doll in her hand, her mouth open as she gazes upward at the enigmatic presence of Uncle Asa, the About-to-Vanish.

We chat and conviviate, warm by grace of the realization that we are not permanently welded to one another, and may value one another in our mutual evanescence.

Late in the evening, Roy confides to me that it really is all working out for the best "because," he explains, "I think I drink too much beer with you around, Asa. You know, you kind of bring out the thirst in me. You get a beer, and first thing you know, there's one in my hand, too."

"You *are* getting a belly, as a matter of fact," I tell him.

Roy bends his head down and pats his stomach comfortably. He is now quasi-naked in his undershirt, shorts, and socks. He is now in his natural state. For he was surely born thus.

"Yes," he says meditatively, "I guess maybe I am."

42

Few truths, Asa Bean the Aphorist says, can be expressed either by the full masculine voice or by subtle feminine silence: rather it is briefly, transiently, upon the swift lip of ambiguity that the utterance of truth can be (ambiguously, swiftly, elusively) heard.

From this sententious circumlocution, then, we arrive at a deeper, swifter, more elusive truth: it is by means of language that we escape the confinement of language. Every poet since the beginning of time has shown us how this is so, for the heuristic discovery that is the very life of a poem is precisely an extension of the commodious skin of language to incorporate new bloods, new vital meats.

All along, during my pilgrimage, Madge Hunter has been the one: the Antagonist, the Unscrupulous, Beautiful, Desired Adversary, plotting my frustration in this Manichean drama upon the theme of Lust and Salvation. She, my Deianira; I, her Hercules.

David Hume understood us when he wrote of subject (male) and object (female), and the Indo-European grammarians knew us as subject (male) and predicate (female). Oh, what realities we compose! Oh, what sentences we write!

God Himself was spawned by our grammars, for how

could God create beyond the purview of syntax? And what exalted principle of good is possible beyond the taxing of sin?

A Sabine virgin, raped in the analects of history, was no more vulnerable to intellectual rape than the fertile mind of this Holy Confusion is open to the rain of possibility!

Discovery: St. Asa Redivivus is one and the same with St. Asa Recidivus.

The world has been waiting for this news, being a fertile field in itself, for Aristotle told us, "All men by nature (*phusis*) desire to know."

Oh, if the world has already discovered this, St. Asa, then your life has been lived in vein. That is, you belong to the great arterial, eternally frustrated majority after all, intent upon the long concatenation of discoveries of truisms that luster their glories in the midnight of our erroneous convictions.

A sublime fortuity casts its holy light upon our endeavors, a pointillism of fact, creating a sublime flow of tone.

A. Sublime pontificates upon the adventitious, creating the essences of essences.

Poikilothermous in a world of (now warm, now cold) ideational flux, I sit upon the Ferris wheel and watch myself turn around and around, and let the animals in my mind frolic beneath my two motionless feet.

Oh, Asa, is it not fun to be smart?

Is it not intellectual to tolerate the transactional observe of one's intellect?

Let the animals play.

I will write another article for Madge. I will breed upon her. Love.

Like that on Deianira's robe, this one, too, may be graced by eluding the vulgar entelechy of communication.

A veil.

176